봄밤

도서출판 아시아에서는 《바이링궐 에디션 한국 대표 소설》을 기획하여 한국의 우수한 문학을 주제별로 엄선해 국내외 독자들에게 소개합니다. 이 기획은 국내외 우수한 번역가들이 참여하여 원작의 품격을 최대한 살렸습니다. 문학을 통해 아시아의 정체성과 가치를 살피는 데 주력해 온 도서출판 아시아는 한국인의 삶을 넓고 깊게 이해하는 데 이 기획이 기여하기를 기대합니다.

Asia Publishers presents some of the very best modern Korean literature to readers worldwide through its new Korean literature series 〈Bilingual Edition Modern Korean Literature〉. We are proud and happy to offer it in the most authoritative translation by renowned translators of Korean literature. We hope that this series helps to build solid bridges between citizens of the world and Koreans through a rich in-depth understanding of Korea.

바이링궐 에디션 한국 대표 소설 055
Bi-lingual Edition Modern Korean Literature 055

Spring Night

권여선
봄밤

Kwon Yeo-sun

ASIA
PUBLISHERS

Contents

봄밤 007
Spring Night

해설 089
Afterword

비평의 목소리 105
Critical Acclaim

작가 소개 114
About the Author

봄밤

Spring Night

"산다는 게 참 끔찍하다. 그렇지 않니?"

영선은 이렇게 말하고 영미를 돌아보았다. 영미는 운전대를 잡고 눈을 가늘게 뜬 채 앞만 바라보고 있었다. 영선이 잠시 기다렸지만 대답이 없었다.

"지난번 면회에서 걔가 우리를 아주 잡아먹으려고 했을 때부터 알아봤어야 하는 건데. 다른 사람은 몰라도 수환이까지 잊어버리다니, 걔가 어떻게 수환이를……"

말하는 도중에 영선은 차가 갑자기 속도를 내는 걸 느꼈다. 커브를 돌 때 그녀는 중심을 잡지 못해 다급히 창문 위 손잡이를 부여잡았다.

"영미야! 속도 좀 늦춰!"

"Life's an awful business, isn't it?"

Yeong-seon turned towards Yeong-mi. Yeong-mi held the steering wheel and narrowed her eyes. She continued to look straight ahead. Yeong-seon waited in vain for Yeong-mi's response for a few moments.

"We should have known what was going on when she acted so aggressively towards us last time we visited her. She... forgetting even Su-hwan! She can forget everyone else, but how could she even forget Su-hwan..."

Yeong-seon felt the car suddenly speed up. When the car turned the corner, she had to scramble to grab a handle over her side of the window

속도는 조금 늦춰졌지만 영선에게는 여전히 빠른 것처럼 생각되었다. 국도변 나무들이 휙휙 지나갔다. 영선은 가슴에 손을 얹었다.

"아이고, 하나님아버지! 얻어 타고 다니는 내가 무슨 말을 하겠니?"

영선이 보란 듯이 안전벨트를 바짝 조여 맸지만 영미는 여전히 눈을 가늘게 뜬 채 앞만 응시하고 있었다.

"너도 낼모레면 환갑인데 운전할 때 그렇게 흥분하는 거 아니다."

영선은 마지막으로 이렇게 오금을 박은 뒤 열선이 켜진 좌석에 몸을 기댔다. 기대도 하지 않았는데 영미가 불쑥 말을 꺼냈다.

"뭘 더 바라겠어?"

영선은 영미를 힐끗 보고 잠시 생각에 잠겼다. 그리고 고개를 끄덕였다.

"그래, 네 말도 맞다. 차라리 잘 된 일인지도 모르지. 어쨌든 더는 나가서 술 먹고 돌아다니진 못할 테니까."

"내 말은, 언니하고 나하고……"

영미의 말에 영선이 좌석에서 몸을 일으켰다.

"그래, 우리가 뭐? 앞으로 우리가 어떻게 해야겠니?

to balance herself.

"Yeong-mi, please slow down!"

Although Yeong-mi slowed down a little, the car still felt like it was going very fast to Yeong-seon. The trees lining the national road passed by quickly. Yeong-seon put a hand to her chest.

"Goodness gracious! What say do I have, since I'm the one getting a ride from you?"

Although Yeong-seon tightened her seat belt as if to protest, Yeong-mi still stared at the road ahead of her, her eyes narrowed.

"You're almost sixty now. You shouldn't drive so fast even when you get upset," Yeong-seon said decisively at last, leaning back against her heated seat.

Unexpectedly, Yeong-mi answered, "What more should we hope for?"

Yeong-seon glanced at Yeong-mi and fell into thoughtful silence. Then, nodding, she said, "Yes, you're right. It may be better this way. Anyway, she can't go out anymore and drink around."

"I mean, what more should we hope for, you and me..." Yeong-mi said.

Yeong-seon sat up straight and said, "Yes, what about us? What should we do? Perhaps we should

영경이 아파트도 팔아버리는 게 좋겠지? 물려줄 자식도 없는 거나 마찬가지니까."

영미가 답답하다는 듯 고개를 빠르게 저었다.

"우리가 뭐 어떻게 할 건 하나도 없고, 어쨌든 우리는 이렇게 멀쩡히 살아 있으니 됐지 않냐고? 뭘 더 바라겠냐고?"

영미의 말을 끝으로 차 안은 엔진 소리와 스쳐가는 바람 소리 외엔 조용했다. 바깥 공기는 아직 쌀쌀한데도 차창으로 쏟아져 들어오는 봄볕은 따스했다.

수환과 영경은 12년 전 마흔셋 봄에 작은 웨딩홀에서 처음 만났다. 수환은 신랑의 고등학교 동창이었고 영경은 신부의 대학교 동창이었다. 신랑신부가 마흔을 훌쩍 넘긴 나이인 데다 쌍방이 모두 재혼이었기에 식은 매우 조촐하게 진행되었다. 하객은 양쪽을 합쳐 50명이 넘지 않았다. 중년의 신랑신부는 신혼여행도 떠나지 않았다. 그들은 마치 재혼의 목적이 거기 있기라도 한 듯 식이 끝나자마자 양쪽 친구들을 자신들의 집에 모아놓고 술을 퍼마시기 시작했다. 술자리는 다음 날 새벽까지 이어졌다.

sell Yeong-gyeong's apartment? It's like she doesn't have any child to give it to.

Yeong-mi immediately shook her head impatiently and said, "There's nothing for us to do. And anyway, shouldn't we be satisfied since we're living fine like this, shouldn't we? What more should we wish for?" Except for the sound of the engine and the sound of the wind passing by outside, it was quiet inside the car. Although the air outside was still cold, the spring sunrays poured warmly into the car.

Su-hwan and Yeong-gyeong met at a small wedding hall in spring twelve years ago when they were both forty-two. Su-hwan was the groom's high school friend and Yeong-gyeong was the bride's college friend. As both bride and groom were well into their forties and this was their second marriage, they were having a small wedding ceremony. The number of guests was less than fifty altogether. The middle-aged bride and groom had decided not to go on a honeymoon, either. As soon as the ceremony ended, they invited their friends to their house and began drinking as if that was the purpose of their wedding. They ended up

새벽에 수환은 술이 억병으로 취한 영경을 업어서 집까지 바래다주었다. 다음날부터 그들은 매일 만나 함께 저녁을 먹고 술을 마셨다. 수환이 술을 잘 먹지 못했으므로 술자리는 늘 영경이 술을 먹고 만취해서 뻗는 걸로 끝났다. 그러면 수환은 첫날 그랬던 것처럼 영경을 업어 그녀의 아파트까지 데려다주었다. 그 번거로운 과정은 일주일 만에 수환이 옥탑방을 정리하고 영경의 아파트로 들어오면서 자연스레 해결되었다. 그 후 그들은 딱 한 번 빼고는 떨어져 살아본 적이 없었다.

면회실로 들어선 영경은 소파에 혼자 앉아 있는 기순을 발견하고 그쪽으로 휠체어를 밀고 갔다. 영경은 수환이 탄 휠체어를 기순의 소파 옆에 고정시키고 자신은 기순과 마주보는 자리에 앉았다.

"어여 와라, 어여 와."

틀니를 하여 발음이 정확하지 않은 기순의 말을 알아듣기 위해 수환은 왼쪽으로 상체를 기울였다.

"밥은 먹었냐?"

기순이 어물거리는 소리로 물었다.

"먹었지, 그럼."

drinking until the wee hours of the next morning. Early the next morning, Su-hwan piggybacked the comatose Yeong-gyeong to her house. From the next day on, they met everyday to have dinner and drink together. As Su-hwan could not drink well, their drinking always ended with Yeong-gyeong completely drunken and spent. Then, Su-hwan always piggybacked Yeong-gyeong and took her to her apartment as he had done the day when they first met. This troublesome process naturally resolved itself as soon as Su-hwan left his rooftop studio and moved in with Yeong-gyeong. Since then, they lived together except for one period of time.

As she entered the visiting room, Yeong-gyeong spotted Gi-sun sitting alone on a sofa and pushed Su-hwan's wheelchair towards her. After parking the wheelchair next to Gi-sun's sofa, Yeong-gyeong took a seat across from Gi-sun.

"So good to see you, my dear, so good!" said Gi-sun.

In order to understand Gi-sun, who spoke in a garbled voice because of her dentures, Su-hwan leaned towards his left side.

수환이 말했다.

"밥은 잘 주냐?"

"그럼 잘 주지."

기순이 이번엔 영경을 보고 물었다.

"아가, 너도 밥은 먹었냐?"

"네, 먹었어요."

"그래, 아가, 너는 몸이 약해서 밥을 많이 먹어야 한다."

영경의 귀에 정확히 그렇게 들린 건 아니었지만 대충 그런 말일 터이므로 영경은 고개를 끄덕였다.

"네, 어머니."

수환이 천천히 고개를 돌려 주변을 돌아보았다.

"형은 이디 갔이?"

기순은 잘 알아듣지 못했다.

"뭐라고?"

수환이 목소리를 높였다.

"형은, 어디, 갔냐고?"

"응. 네 형은 담배 피우러 나갔어. 곧 들어올 거야. 아직도 못 끊고 저런다."

수환은 수철이 곧 들어오지 않으리라는 것을 알고 있

"Have you eaten yet?" Gi-sun asked, still mumbling.

"Of course, mom," Su-hwan said.

"Was the food decent?"

"Of course."

Gi-sun turned towards Yeong-gyeong and asked, "Have you eaten yet, too, dear?"

"Yes, mother."

"Good, my dear. You have to eat a lot, because your body is weak."

Although Yeong-gyeong could not exactly make out Gi-sun's words, she supposed their meaning and answered, nodding her head in recognition, "Yes, mother."

Su-hwan turned his head and slowly looked around the room. "Where is Brother?" he asked.

Unable to make out Su-hwan's words, Gi-sun asked, "What did you say?"

Su-hwan raised his voice, "Brother. Where is Brother?"

"Oh, he went out to smoke. He'll come in soon. He still hasn't quit smoking."

Su-hwan knew that Su-cheol wouldn't come in, but he said nothing. As if to say that this was the right timing, Gi-sun took Su-hwan's left hand with

었지만 아무 말도 하지 않았다. 기순은 드디어 때가 왔다는 듯 검버섯으로 뒤덮인 두 손으로 수환의 왼손을 꼭 붙들고 울기 시작했다.

"아이고, 수환아, 우리 수환이, 불쌍한 우리 수환이……"

기순은 한동안 울었다. 수환은 기순에게 손을 잡힌 채 영경을 보았다. 영경은 멍한 눈빛으로 기순의 위쪽 허공을 바라보고 있었다.

"우리 엄마, 기운 빠지신다. 그만해."

수환이 슬그머니 손을 뺐다. 기순이 주머니에서 거즈 손수건을 꺼내 눈곱을 닦으며 말했다.

"내가 밥만 끓여먹을 수 있으면 요 근처에 방 얻어가지고 살면서 매일 와서 너를 이렇게 만져볼 것을."

"말도 안 되는 소리 하지 마. 형이 그러라고 하겠어?"

"네 형이 말도 못 꺼내게 해."

시무룩하던 기순이 갑자기 눈을 번득이며 말했다.

"이게 다 환이 네가 쇠를 많이 만져 이렇게 된 거다."

뻔한 레퍼토리였지만 수환은 진지하게 대꾸했다.

"그건 아니라니까."

"뭐가 아니야? 젊어서부터 쇠 깎고 불질을 해서 그런

her both hands and began crying.

"Oh dear, my dear Su-hwan, my poor Su-hwan..."

Gi-sun cried for a while. His hand in Gi-sun's hands, Su-hwan looked at Yeong-gyeong. Yeong-gyeong was staring blankly upwards in the air.

"Mom, you'll be exhausted. Please stop crying," Su-hwan said and slipped his hand out of her grasp. Taking her gauze handkerchief out of her pocket and wiping away the gunk from her eyes, Gi-sun said, "If only I could boil rice, I would rent a room nearby and come to see you and hold you every day."

"Nonsense! Do you think Brother would let you?"

"Your brother doesn't even let me begin to discuss it," Gi-sun said sullenly.

Suddenly, Gi-sun announced, her eyes brightening up, "This is all because you handled too much iron."

Although this was a dreary routine, Su-hwan responded sincerely, "That's not true."

"Why not? It's because you cut and burnt iron ever since you were young."

"No. That causes another illness. Mine is something else."

거야."

기순이 분연히 말했다.

"아니야. 그래서 생기는 병은 따로 있고 나는 그 병이 아니라니까."

"다들 그러더라. 몸에 쇳독이 올라서 병이 난 거라고. 안 그러면 젊은 나이에 왜 이런 병에 걸려?"

"엄마, 나 안 젊어."

수환은 웃으며 영경을 보았다.

"쉰다섯이 왜 안 젊어? 공장 차려놓고 쇠 만지고 불질 안 했으면 네가 왜 이런 병에 걸려? 눈에 아다리 걸려가면서 그 힘든 일 해서 다 남 좋은 일만 시키고. 아이고, 내가 그년을 어디서라도 만나면 요절을 내도 시원찮다만은."

기순의 분명치 않은 넋두리를 들으며 수환은 계속 영경을 바라보았다. 영경은 똑같은 표정이었다. 수환이 가장 잘 알고 있고 가장 두려워하는, 넋이 나간 듯 텅 비어 있는 가면의 표정……

수철은 오전 면회 시간이 다 끝나갈 때쯤에야 들어와 말없이 기순의 뒤에 서 있다가 면회종료 벨이 울리자 다시 울먹이기 시작하는 기순을 일으켜 세웠다. 무표정

"Everyone says that the poison from the irons made you sick. If it wasn't that, how could you have caught this kind of illness when you were so young?"

"Mom, I'm not young." Su-hwan looked at Yeong-gyeong smiling.

"Why, isn't fifty-five young? If you hadn't set up that shop to handle and fire iron, why would you have caught this kind of disease? Working so hard that you ended up ruining your eyes and getting taken advantage of. Oh, if I run into that bitch and break her now, that still wouldn't be enough!" As he listened to Gi-sun's inarticulate grumbling, Su-hwan kept an eye on Yeong-gyeong. Yeong-gyeong's face remained the same. She wore a blank, mask-like expression that Su-hwan knew well and was afraid of.

Su-cheol came back when the interview was almost over and stood silently behind Gi-sun. and then helped her stand up when the bell rang. Gi-sun began to cry again. Surprised at the sound of the bell, Yeong-gyeong awoke from her stupor and stood up, too. Su-cheol took Gi-sun from visiting room and Yeong-gyeong followed them, pushing Su-hwan's wheelchair along with him. At

하게 앉아 있던 영경도 벨소리를 듣자 놀라서 자리에서 일어났다. 수철이 기순을 데리고 면회실을 나갔고 영경이 수환의 휠체어를 밀고 그 뒤를 따랐다. 본관의 현관 입구에서 수환은 환갑 넘은 형이 여든 넘은 노모를 10년도 더 된 낡은 자동차의 뒷좌석에 태우고 요양원 정문을 빠져나가는 걸 바라보았다.

수환에게 류마티스 관절염으로 의심되는 증상이 나타난 것은 3년 또는 3년 반 전이었다. 그러나 신용불량 상태로 15년 가까이 살아온 수환은 건강보험에 가입되어 있지 않았으므로 곧바로 병원에 가볼 수 없었다. 어쩔 수 없는 일 앞에서 누구나 그러하듯, 수환도 크게 염려하지 않고 사태를 낙관하는 걸로 영경과 자신의 불안을 잠재웠다. 1년쯤 지나자 수환은 도저히 더는 이렇게 버틸 수 없다는 판단을 내렸다. 그는 오래 전에 영경을 처음 만났던 그 자그마한 웨딩홀에서 재혼한 고등학교 동창에게 전화를 걸었다. 건강보험증을 빌려줄 수 없겠냐는 그의 부탁에 친구는 낄낄 웃으면서 요즘은 보험증 같은 건 필요 없고 병원에 가서 이름과 주민번호만 대면 된다고 흔쾌히 자신의 주민번호를 알려주었다.

the entrance of the main building, Su-hwan watched his brother, well into his sixties, help his mother, in her eighties, get into the back seat of his more than ten-year old car and leave through the nursing home gate.

It had been three or three and half years ago since Su-hwan began suffering from symptoms suspicious of rheumatoid arthritis. But, having lived for more than ten years with a bad credit rating, Su-hwan did not take care to update his health insurance policy, and therefore could not go to the hospital immediately. Like anyone who must face something inevitable, Su-hwan tried to calm his, as well as Yeong-gyeong's worries down simply by remaining optimistic. About a year later, Su-hwan realized that he could not go on like this any longer. He called his high school friend who had remarried at the small wedding hall where he had met Yeong-gyeong for the first time. When Su-hwan asked if he could borrow his friend's health insurance card, his friend giggled and gave Su-hwan his resident registration number, saying that these days one did not need the insurance card at the hospital, but only his name and resident regis-

동네병원 의사는 간단한 검사를 한 후 수환에게 당장 큰 병원에 가보는 게 좋겠다고 말했다. 하지만 큰 병원에 가면 백발백중 복잡한 검사와 수술을 받아야 할 텐데 친구의 건강보험으로 그렇게 할 수는 없었다. 수환은 동네병원에서 해줄 수 있는 처치와 처방은 없는지 물었다. 의사는 간단한 파라핀 치료와 일반적인 류마티즘 약을 처방할 수는 있지만 이미 비틀리기 시작한 관절 상태로 보아 큰 효과를 기대하기는 어려울 거라고 말했다. 하지만 수환은 당분간 그렇게라도 치료를 받아보기로 했다. 처음에는 증상이 한결 완화되는 느낌이 들었다. 하지만 몇 달 뒤에는 상태가 걷잡을 수 없이 악화되었다.

영선과 영미는 혼자 면회실로 들어오는 영경을 보고 나란히 소파에서 일어났다. 영경은 그들 맞은편 소파에 앉아 탁자 위에 펼쳐진 음식을 흘깃 보더니 말없이 창문 쪽으로 고개를 돌렸다. 영경의 비참한 몰골에 영선과 영미는 어찌해야 좋을지 몰라 서로 얼굴을 마주보았다. 먼저 말을 꺼낸 건 영미였다.

"뭐 좀 안 먹을래, 막내야?"

tration number.

After a simple test, the doctor at a small neighborhood clinic told Su-hwan to leave immediately for a large hospital. But, since going to a large hospital would no doubt mean complicated tests and operations, Su-hwan could not afford to do that on his friend's health insurance alone. Su-hwan asked if there was any treatment and medication option the doctor could recommend to him. The doctor said that Su-hwan could try a simple paraffin treatment and general rheumatism medication, but that he was doubtful about their effectiveness given Su-hwan's already distorted joints. Nevertheless, Su-hwan decided to try this option for the time being. At first, his symptoms seemed to be easing a lot, but they began to worsen quickly after a few months.

Yeong-seon and Yeong-mi stood up at the same time when they saw Yeong-gyeong enter the visiting room alone. Yeong-gyeong sat down on the sofa across from them, and, after glancing at the food spread on the table, she turned her head towards the window without a word. Not knowing what to say after looking at Yeong-gyeong's piti-

영경은 고개를 저었다.

"수환 씨는 어때?"

"그냥 그래."

영경은 창밖을 보며 건성으로 대답했다.

"더 나빠지진 않았어?"

영경은 그거 아주 훌륭한 질문이라는 듯 고개를 돌려 두 언니들을 차례로 보았다.

"어떻게 더 안 나빠지겠어? 원래 나빠지기 시작하면 걷잡을 수 없는 병이라는데."

그 병에 대해서라면 듣기도 지겹다는 듯 영선이 체머리를 흔들자 영경은 그걸 놓치지 않았다.

"큰언니는 그럴 거면 여기 뭐하러 왔어?"

영선이 황급히 표정을 바꾸었다.

"뭐하러 오긴? 널 보러 왔지."

영경이 웃었다.

"큰언니도 늙었는지 연기에 진실성 없는 거 티 나요."

"그러지 마, 영경아. 언니도 정말 네 걱정 많이 해."

영미가 말했다.

"작은언니, 그러니까 제발 집에서 걱정만 하라고. 이렇게 와서 벌 서지들 말고."

able shape, Yeong-seon and Yeong-mi looked at each other wordlessly as well. Finally, Yeong-mi said, "Won't you eat something, dear?"

Yeong-gyeong shook her head.

"How is Su-hwan?"

"So-so," Yeong-gyeong answered without much thought, looking out the window.

"He hasn't gotten worse?"

As if this was a welcome question, Yeong-gyeong turned towards her elder sisters and looked at them, moving slowly from one face to the next.

"How could he not get worse? They say it's an illness that quickly worsens once it really begins." Yeong-seon shook her head as if to say that she was tired of even hearing about Su-hwan's illness. Yeong-gyeong did not miss it.

"Why did you come here if you were going to be this way?" Yeong-gyeong asked.

Yeong-seon quickly changed her expression and said, "Why did I come? I came to see you, of course."

Yeong-gyeong smiled and said, "You must have gotten old. Your acting gives you away."

"Don't be this way, Yeong-gyeong. She really

"영경이 너 진짜 점점."

영선이 혀를 찼다.

"큰언니, 말씀 한번 잘하셨어. 내가 진짜 점점 뭐?"

"여기 직원한테 들었는데 너 지난번에 나가서 일주일이나 있다가 들어왔다며? 들어온 지 보름밖에 안 됐다며? 보름 만에 벌써 이러는 거니? 네가 그렇게 끔찍이 생각하는 수환이를 봐서라도 이러면 안 되는 거 아니니?"

영경이 다시 창 쪽으로 고개를 돌리자 영선과 영미는 다시 얼굴을 마주보았다. 영미가 그러지 말라는 눈짓을 하자 영선이 마지못해 고개를 끄덕였다. 영경이 넋두리하듯 중얼거렸다.

"보름밖에, 보름밖에라. 그게 아닌 거거든, 내 지랄병은. 보름씩이나인 거거든."

영경은 잠시 입을 꾹 다물고 있다 갑자기 무슨 좋은 생각이라도 떠오른 듯 언니들 쪽으로 고개를 돌렸다.

"가만 있어봐."

영경의 말에 영미가 몸을 앞으로 내밀었다.

"왜, 막내야? 얘기해."

"그러니까……"

worries about you," Yeong-mi said.

"So, please stay home and just worry about me. Don't come here to be self-punished."

"Yeong-gyeong, you, really..." Yeong-seon clucked her tongue.

"Well said. So I, really, what?"

"I heard from the staff member here that you went out for a week. Is that right? It was only after two weeks since you came in, right? Only two weeks? Shouldn't you try not to behave like that, if you're really thinking of Su-hwan?"

Yeong-gyeong turned her head towards the window again and Yeong-seon and Yeong-mi looked at each other. Yeong-mi motioned to Yeong-seon to drop the subject, and Yeong-seon nodded reluctantly.

Yeong-gyeong grumbled, "Only two weeks, only two weeks. But that's false as far as my crazy fit is concerned. It's more like, two *whole* weeks."

Yeong-gyeong then shut her lips tight until she abruptly whirled towards her sisters as if she had come upon a great idea. "Wait a minute."

Yeong-mi leaned forward and said, "What is it, dear? Tell us."

"Let's see..." Yeong-gyeong grumbled. "If I was

영경이 낮게 으르렁거렸다.

"내가 일주일 나가 있었고 들어온 지 보름 됐으면 언니들은 대체 얼마 만에 온 거니?"

영미가 죄인처럼 손을 모았다.

"막내야, 그동안 내가 좀 아팠어. 그래서 못 왔어. 큰언니는 와보고 싶어 했는데 내가 운전을 못해서 그렇게 됐어. 미안해."

영경이 하하 웃었다. 영미와 영선도 덩달아 억지로 미소를 지었다.

"늘 그랬지. 그때도 그랬지. 늘 언니들은 옳고 이유가 있지. 그만 가세요들."

영경이 자리에서 벌떡 일어서자 영미가 덩달아 일어서려다 얕은 비명을 터뜨리며 무릎을 움켜쥐었다.

"막내야, 잠깐만. 막내야, 그러지 마. 큰언니도 많이 늙었어. 힘든 걸음 한 거야."

"네, 그러셔요? 작은언니 그 무릎으로 운전하느라 얼마나 힘드셨어요? 그 차에 실려 오느라 큰언니는 또 얼마나 힘드셨어요? 어쩌다 생각나면 몰려와서 사람 더 돌게 만들지 말고 그만 가시라고요. 여기가 도시락 싸가지고 소풍 오는 데는 아니……"

out for a week and this happened two weeks after I was admitted here, then how long did it take for you to come visit me?" Yeong-mi clasped her hands as if from a guilty conscience. "Deary, I was sick for a while. That's why I couldn't come. Big sister wanted to visit you, but I couldn't drive. I'm sorry."

Yeong-gyeong laughed out loud. Yeong-mi and Yeong-seon forced smiles.

"It has always been like this. It was like this then, too," Yeong-gyeong mused. "You were always right and you always had the right reasons. Go away."

Yeong-gyeong abruptly stood up then. Yeong-mi was getting up automatically when she grabbed her knees with a soft cry.

"Dear, wait a minute, dear. Don't be this way. Big sister is old now. This wasn't easy for her," Yeong-mi said.

"Oh, yes? Oh, how hard it was for you to drive with your knees like that? How hard was it for you, Big Sister, to get a ride from her? Don't make a big deal about visiting me because you occasionally feel like it. Just go now. This isn't a place for a picnic..."

영경이 목이 막혀 말을 멈추자 영미의 눈시울이 붉어졌다.

"작은언니, 가! 큰언니, 가! 가라고! 욕 나오기 전에."

영경의 개 쫓는 듯한 말투와 손짓에 놀라 영선이 가슴에 손을 얹고 탄식했다.

"아이고, 하나님아버지! 저런 게 학교에서 애들을 가르쳤다니."

면회실 문을 향해 걸어가는 영경의 귀에 영미의 가느다란 외침이 들려왔다.

"막내야, 기도해! 언니도 기도할게. 하나님은 너를 사랑하셔! 영원히……"

건강보험에 가입하기 위해 수환은 영경과 의논하여 신용회복 절차를 밟기로 했다. 그는 자신이 진 빚이 얼마인지는 대충 알고 있었지만 갚아야 할 빚이 얼마인지는 전혀 알지 못했다. 세월은 양면을 가지고 있어, 세월이 많이 흘러 이자도 그만큼 엄청나게 불어났겠지만 또 세월이 많이 흘러 빚이 이미 불량채권이 되어버렸을 가능성도 높았다. 수환은 후자의 경우를 바랐지만 여러 가지 복잡한 법적 문제가 얽혀 있어 그의 부채 액수는

Yeong-gyeong choked up and couldn't continue. Yeong-mi's eyes reddened.

"Go, Sister! Go, Big Sister! Go! Go! Before I really get going!"

Yeong-gyeong sounded as if she was kicking out a pair of dogs. Surprised by Yeong-gyeong's words and attitude, Yeong-seon sighed and said, with her hands on her chest, "Goodness Gracious! This is the behavior of a teacher who used to teach children at school!"

Walking towards the visiting room door, Yeong-gyeong could hear Yeong-mi softly cry, "Dear, pray! I'll pray, too. God loves you! Forever..."

In order to apply for health insurance, Su-hwan decided to take steps to recover his credit after discussing it with Yeong-gyeong. He knew how much he had borrowed, but he didn't know how much he had to repay. Time's face had two sides. After such a long time, the interest could have grown enormously, but the debt itself might have become delinquent. Su-hwan hoped that the latter was the case, but it turned out most his debt had not been forgiven due to various complicated legal reasons.

거의 탕감되지 않았다.

수환은 영경과 다시 의논하여 신용을 회복하는 대신 파산을 신청하기로 했다. 파산신청을 해도 건강보험에는 가입할 수 있다고 했다. 파산선고가 내려진 후 그들은 결혼신고를 하고 같은 건강보험증을 갖게 되었지만 그동안 수환의 증상은 급속히 악화되었다. 마침내 수환이 종합병원의 진료를 받을 수 있게 되었을 때는 염증이 척추까지 침범해 혼자서는 제대로 걸을 수 없는 상태였다. 게다가 병원에 입원하자마자 기다렸다는 듯 온갖 합병증이 발병했다.

1년 전에 수환은 영경과 의논하여 병원치료를 포기하고 노인과 중증환자들을 전문으로 돌봐주는 지방요양원에 입주했다. 시설이 괜찮은 곳이라 입주금이 적잖게 들었지만 다행히 그 정도는 영경의 저금으로 충당할 수 있었다. 영경은 서울 아파트에, 수환은 지방요양원에 각자 두 달 정도 떨어져 지냈는데, 그게 그들이 12년의 동거생활 중 유일하게 떨어져 살아본 시기였다.

영경은 병실 창가에 서서 본관 뒤뜰을 내려다보고 있었다.

Su-hwan discussed the matter with Yeong-gyeong again and decided that he should file for bankruptcy. A bankrupt person would be allowed health insurance. After applying for bankruptcy, they married and could finally subscribe to the same health insurance policy. But Su-hwan's symptoms had deteriorated rapidly in the mean time. When Su-hwan finally got to the big hospital, he couldn't even walk alone because the inflammation had transferred to his spine. In addition, as soon as he had been hospitalized, he developed all kinds of complications as if they had been waiting for that day.

A year ago, Su-hwan gave up on hospital treatment and entered a country nursing home for the elderly and patients with serious illnesses. It was a home with nice facilities, and so it cost a considerable amount to enter. Luckily, Yeong-gyeong had had enough savings. For two months, Yeong-gyeong lived in their apartment in Seoul and Su-hwan lived in the country nursing home. That was the only time they lived apart from each other during their twelve years living together.

Yeong-gyeong was standing behind a window

"기분 안 좋아?"

병상에 비스듬히 누운 수환이 물었다.

"아니야."

영경은 고개도 돌리지 않고 말했다.

"면회는 잘 했어? 언니들은 어떠셔?"

"뭘 어때? 늘 그렇지."

"건강하시지?"

"내가 알 게 뭐야? 건강하겠지."

"왜 남 말 하듯 해? 언니들도 나이가 있으신데 어디 건강하시기만 하겠어?"

"그래, 작은언니도 무릎이 많이 아픈 것 같더라. 큰언니야 늘 심장이 안 좋은 데다 머리도 아프고 백내장에 뭐에 여러 가지로 복잡하게 아프지. 근데 우리 주제에 그런 거 걱정할 때니?"

수환은 할 말이 없었다. 영경은 뒤뜰 쪽으로 휠체어를 밀고 가는 늙은 여자의 뒷모습을 내려다보았다. 휠체어에 탄 사람은 보이지 않았지만 아마 늙은 남자일 거라고 그녀는 생각했다.

"내 안부도 전해주지. 언니들이 뭐라셔?"

수환이 잠긴 목소리로 물었다.

and looking down on the back yard behind the main building.

"What's the matter?" Su-hwan asked, lying obliquely on his hospital bed.

"Nothing," Yeong-gyeong said, without turning around.

"How was your time with your sisters? What are they up to?"

"Nothing in particular. They're the same."

"Healthy?"

"How should I know? I guess they are."

"Why are you talking about them like they're strangers? Your sisters are old now, so they can't just be healthy, right?"

"That's true. Yeong-mi seemed to have a lot of pain in her knees. Big sister has many troubles, as you know. Her heart isn't well. She suffers from headaches. She has a cataract. But, do we have time to worry about their health?"

Su-hwan had nothing to say. Yeong-gyeong could see the back of an old woman push a wheelchair towards the back yard. Although she could not see the person sitting on the wheelchair, Yeong-gyeong assumed that he was an elderly man.

"뭐래긴 뭐래? 늘 똑같은 소리지."

"우리 엄마도 늘 똑같은 소리 하시잖아?"

"그 소리랑 그 소리가 같니?"

"우리 형을 봐. 부모하고 형제는 다른 거야."

"우리 환이 도가 트셨구나."

"기분 안 좋네, 우리 빵경이."

"아니야."

"그럼 나 봐야지."

"당신이 자꾸 모르는 소리를 하니까……"

영경이 돌아섰다.

"그러다 또 울겠네."

수환이 뻣뻣한 손을 움직여 가까이 오라는 손짓을 하자 영경은 그의 병상 옆으로 와서 눈을 내리깔았다. 오전 면회 때 기순이 붙들고 울던, 제멋대로 자란 관목처럼 굽고 흰 그의 손가락 위로 눈물이 후두둑 떨어졌다.

"이거 슬퍼서 우는 거 아닌 거 알지?"

영경이 말했다.

"난 슬퍼도 못 우는 거 알지?"

수환이 말했다.

"참 장한 커플이다, 우리."

"Did you say hello to them from me? What were they talking about?" Su-hwan asked, her voice low and hoarse.

"What would they say? Always the same thing."

"My mom says always the same thing, doesn't she?"

"Do you think what your mom says and what my sisters say are the same?"

"Look at my big brother. Parents and siblings are different."

"Huh, you've become spiritually enlightened, Hwan!"

"You aren't feeling well, my Bbang-gyeong!"

"Not really."

"Then, you should be looking at me."

"It's because you're so clueless..."

Yeong-gyeong turned around.

"You look like you are about to cry," Su-hwan said.

Su-hwan stiffly motioned to Yeong-gyeong to come closer. Yeong-gyeong approached, her eyes downcast. Tears fell onto Su-hwan's bent, distorted fingers, fingers like bushes grown at random, fingers that Gi-sun had clasped and cried over.

"You know I'm not crying because I'm sad, right?"

"맞아. 당신 참 장해. 오래 버텼어. 다녀와라."

영경의 젖은 눈에 퍼뜩 생기가 돌았다.

"정말 괜찮겠어?"

"난 괜찮아."

영경이 더는 묻지 않고 단호한 어조로 말했다.

"다행이다."

"다행이지. 우리 빵경이, 걱정 말고 다녀와."

영경이 눈물을 뚝뚝 흘렸다.

"나 정말 안 나가겠다는 말은 못 하겠어, 환아."

"그래, 다녀오라니까. 너무 오래 있지만 말고."

영경이 눈물을 훔치며 빠르게 말했다.

"오래 안 있어. 사흘, 아니 이틀. 환아, 그 정도면 충분해. 이틀만 있다 들어올게. 딱 두 밤 자고 들어올게, 환아."

그 말을 듣고 수환은 환하게 웃으려고 했다.

수환과 영경이 떨어져 지낸 두 달 동안 수환의 증세도 눈에 띄게 나빠졌지만 영경의 증세는 더욱 나빠졌다. 두 달 후에 영경은 아파트를 반월세로 놓고 보증금 받은 걸로 자기 몫의 입주금을 내고 수환이 있는 요양

Yeong-gyeong said.

"You know I can't even cry at all when I'm sad, right?" Su-hwan answered.

"What an amazing couple we are!"

"That's right. You're amazing. You've been patient for so long. Why don't you step outside just for a while?"

Yeong-gyeong's wet eyes shone.

"Are you sure you're going to be okay?" Yeong-gyeong asked.

"I'm fine."

Yeong-gyeong did not insist, but looked resolute. "That's fortunate."

"That's fortunate. My Bbang-gyeong, don't worry. Take a break for a while."

Tears fell from Yeong-gyeong's eyes.

"I really can't say that I won't go out, Hwan!" Yeong-gyeong said.

"Do, go out. Just don't be too long."

Yeong-gyeong wiped her tears away and said hurriedly, "I won't be long. Three days. No, two days. Hwan, two days is all I need. I'll be back in two days. I'll be back in just two days, Hwan."

Su-hwan tried to smile.

원으로 들어왔다. 영경의 병명은 중증 알코올중독과 간경화, 심각한 영양실조였다. 그렇게 류마티즘 환자와 알코올중독 환자의 위험한 동거가 이곳 요양원에서 시작되었다. 요양원 직원들은 유난히 의가 좋고 사랑스러운 대신 화약처럼 아슬아슬한 그들 부부를 '알루 커플'이라 불렀다.

서로 떨어져 살지 않기 위해 영경이 요양원에 들어왔지만 그 때문에 그들은 이후로 만남과 헤어짐을 반복하지 않으면 안 되었다. 요양원에서는 절대 술을 마실 수 없도록 되어 있었다. 몰래 술을 먹다 두 번이나 걸린 영경은 마지막으로 한 번만 더 적발되면 당장 퇴원조치하겠다는 위협을 받았다. 그래서 영경은 구토와 불면, 경련과 섬망 증상에 시달리다 더 이상 견디기 어려우면 외출증을 끊어 요양원 밖으로 나가 술을 마시고 돌아오곤 했다. 남편인 수환이 그걸 제지하려는 강력한 의지를 보이기는커녕 본인인 영경의 의사를 최우선으로 존중했으므로 담당의도 어찌할 수가 없었다. 영경은 처음엔 당일에 들어왔지만 곧 이틀이 지나 들어왔고 때로는 사흘 만에 들어오기도 했는데, 지난번엔 오후에 면회 온 영선의 말대로 일주일 만에 들어왔다.

During the two months Su-hwan and Yeong-gyeong lived apart, it wasn't just Su-hwan's symptoms that worsened visibly. Yeong-gyeong's symptoms worsened as well. After two months, Yeong-gyeong rented her apartment out in exchange for monthly rent and a large security deposit sum that she used to pay for her fee at the nursing home and move in to the nursing home where Su-hwan was staying. Yeong-gyeong's was diagnosed with a case of serious alcoholism, hepatocirrhosis, and severe malnutrition. This was how the cohabitation of a rheumatism patient and an alcoholic patient began in the nursing home. The nursing home staff called this particularly loving, cute, but precarious couple—as precarious and dangerous as gunpowder—"the al-rheu couple."

Although Yeong-gyeong had entered the nursing home to be with Su-hwan, they had had to part and reunite again and again because she stayed there. Absolutely no alcohol was allowed in the nursing home. Yeong-gyeong had been found drinking secretly twice, and she had been threatened with permanent removal if she was found drinking again. As a result, Yeong-gyeong suffered from nausea, insomnia, spasm, and delirium. She

질병이 다른 만큼 수환과 영경은 담당의도 각기 달랐다. 그러나 두 의사가 한결같이 주장하건대 '알루 커플'은 급작스럽게 악화될 가능성이 높은 고위험 질환을 앓는 환자군에 속했다. 그래서 그들 부부는 요양원 별채가 아닌, 중증환자들을 위한 본관 병동의 숙소에 입주해 있었다.

외출하기 전에 영경은 숙소에서 간단히 가방을 챙긴 후 수환의 담당의를 만나보러 갔다. 마침 의사는 자리를 비우고 없었다. 영경은 기다리려다 슬그머니 돌아섰다. 수환의 상태에 대해 좋지 않은 소리를 듣는 걸 견딜 수 없었다. 어차피 들어도 소용없는 일이었다. 수환이 허락한 한, 그녀가 오늘 외출하는 건 해가 뜨고 해가 지는 것처럼, 아니 그보다 더 굳건하고 완강한 사실이라 도저히 변경될 수 없었다. 영경은 빠른 걸음으로 자신의 담당의를 만나러 갔다. 외출하기 위해서는 수환의 담당의는 만나지 않아도 되지만 자신의 담당의는 반드시 만나야 했다.

영경의 담당의는 늘 하나마나한 소리를 늘어놓았다. 환자 본인의 의지로는 안 되는 일이다, 남편이든 형제든 누군가를 보호자로 내세워 강제 입원을 해야 한다,

got permission to leave and left when she could not endure the symptoms any longer. After drinking for a short while, she would come back. Su-hwan did not show any strong prerogative for her to stop this. Not only that, he respected Yeong-gyeong's decision the most. Yeong-gyeong's doctor was helpless. At first, Yeong-gyeong came back the same day, but she soon would come back on the second, and then, third day. The last time she left, she returned a week later, as Yeong-seon had pointed out during her visit that afternoon.

As Su-hwan and Yeong-gyeong suffered from different illnesses they received the attention of different doctors. Nevertheless, both doctors agreed that the "al-rheu couple" belonged to the group of patients who suffered from illnesses that had a strong possibility of suddenly worsening. As a result, the couple stayed in the main building for intensive care patients, not one of the annex buildings.

Before Yeong-gyeong went out for a leave, she packed her bag and went to see Su-hwan's doctor. The doctor was not in his office. Yeong-gyeong thought of waiting for him, but then turned back

보호자의 동의 없이는 나갈 수 없도록 통제를 해놓고 치료를 해야 한다, 이렇게 들락날락거려서는 아무 효과가 없다 등등 귀에 못이 박이도록 들어온 얘기였다. 영경은 늘 그랬듯이 생각해보겠다고 말했다. 의사는 한숨을 쉬고 외출증에 사인을 해주었다. 영경은 오늘따라 담당의가 왠지 자신에게 적대적이라는 생각을 했지만 어쩌면 그건 자기 병의 또 다른 증상일 수도 있다고 생각했다.

영경이 병실로 돌아왔을 때 수환은 잠자는 듯 보였다. 그러나 영경이 살그머니 다가가 손을 잡자 수환은 눈을 떴다.

"가는 거야?"

"아니."

"그럼 안 가?"

"아니, 좀 있다 막차 시간에 맞춰 나가려고. 그 전에 책 좀 읽어줄까 해서."

"그래."

"괜찮아?"

"응, 괜찮아. 읽어줘."

영경은 가방에서 책과 안경을 꺼냈다. 아주 오래된 세

without saying a word. She could not stand hearing bad news about Su-hwan's health any more. There was nothing she could do anyway. As long as Su-hwan agreed, she was leaving that day. This was a firm and stubborn fact like the sun rising and setting. No, it was a fact even more unchangeable than that. Yeong-gyeong hurried over to see her own doctor. In order to go out for a leave, she had to see her doctor, even if she was not required to see Su-hwan's doctor.

Yeong-gyeong's doctor rattled off the usual lecture. A patient's will alone could not do. A guardian —whoever it might be, her husband or her sibling —had to force her to stay in the nursing home. Her treatment had to be controlled so that she could not leave without her guardian's permission. There was no use treating her if she could come and go at her own will. The usual lecture. As usual, Yeong-gyeong said that she would think it over. Sighing deeply, the doctor signed her form. Yeong-gyeong thought that her doctor seemed more antagonistic towards her today, but she also thought that that feeling of hers might be one of the symptoms of her illness.

When Yeong-gyeong returned to his room, Su-

로 판형의 『부활』이었다.

"아까 재밌는 데를 읽어서 당신한테 읽어주려고 접어 놨지."

"그래, 잘했다."

영경은 왼손으로 오른쪽 팔꿈치를 받쳐 떨리는 손으로 안경을 끼고 책을 수환의 옆구리 쪽 시트에 비스듬히 걸쳐놓았다. 그리고 책의 접어놓은 부분을 펼쳤다.

"어떤 정치범에 대한 톨스토이의 설명이야."

"응."

영경은 손을 더듬어 다시 수환의 손을 잡고 책을 읽기 시작했다.

"노보드보로프는 혁명가들 사이에서 대단한 존경을 받고 있었으며 또 훌륭한 학자이고 아주 현명한 인물이었음에도 불구하고 네흘류도프는 그를 도덕적 자질로 봐서 일반 수준보다 훨씬 하위의 혁명가 부류로 간주했다."

영경은 계속 읽어나갔다. 이름도 발음하기 어려운 노보드보로프라는 혁명가는, 톨스토이에 따르면, 이지력은 남보다 뛰어났지만 자만심 또한 굉장하여 결국 별 쓸모없는 인간이라는 것이었다. 그 까닭인즉, 이지력이

hwan looked as if he was sleeping. But when she approached him and held his hand, he opened his eyes.

"Are you leaving?"

"No."

"You aren't leaving, then?"

"No. I'll leave a little later to catch the last bus. I thought maybe I could read a book for you until then."

"Okay."

"Are you sure?"

"Yes. Please read."

Yeong-gyeong took out a book and a pair of glasses from her bag. It was a very old *Resurrection* printed vertically.

"There was a very interesting part I read a while ago. I dog-eared the page."

"That's great."

Yeong-gyeong put on her glasses with her shaky right hand by supporting her right elbow with her left hand. Then, she propped the book against the sheet covering Su-hwan's side. She opened the book to the page she had dog-eared.

"It's Tolstoy's explanation about a political prisoner."

분자라면 자만심은 분모여서 분자의 숫자가 아무리 크더라도 분모의 숫자가 그보다 측량할 수 없이 더 크게 되면 분자를 초과해버리기 때문이라는 것이었다.

책을 다 읽고 난 영경이 수환을 보았다.

"분자, 분모. 머리에 쏙 박히는 설명이네."

수환이 말했다.

"그렇지? 가끔 톨스토이에게 반하게 되는 이유가 이런 대목 때문인 것 같아."

영경은 여전히 수환의 손을 잡은 채 한 손으로 안경을 빼려고 했다. 손은 안경테를 잡을 듯 말 듯 허공에서 파들거렸다. 며칠 전에 심한 사지경련을 일으킨 후로 그녀는 아직까지 손을 떨고 있었다. 그녀가 잡아채듯 안경을 빼며 말했다.

"내가 생각해봤는데 이 비유는 모든 사람에게 적용시킬 수 있을 것 같아. 분자에 그 사람의 좋은 점을 놓고 분모에 그 사람의 나쁜 점을 놓으면 그 사람의 값이 나오는 식이지. 아무리 장점이 많아도 단점이 더 많으면 그 값은 1보다 작고 그 역이면 1보다 크고."

"그러니까 1이 기준인 거네."

수환이 말했다.

"Okay."

Yeong-gyeong fumbled her hand to hold Su-hwan's and began reading the passage.

"Although Novodvorov was more esteemed than all the other revolutionists, though he was very learned, and considered very wise, Nekhlyudov reckoned him among those of the revolutionists who, being below the average moral level, was very far below it."

Yeong-gyeong continued to read. The revolutionist with a name very hard to pronounce, Novodvorov, according to Tolstoy, was smarter than the others, but he was so arrogant that he was useless. This was because if one's intellectual power is a numerator and his conceit a denominator, the denominator, inestimably larger than the numerator, would completely overwhelm the numerator, no matter how large the numerator might be.

After Yeong-gyeong finished reading the passage, she looked at Su-hwan.

"A numerator and a denominator. A very succinct explanation," Su-hwan said.

"Isn't it? I think it's because of a passage like this that I fall in love with Tolstoy often."

Her one hand still in Su-hwan's hand, Yeong-

"그렇지. 모든 인간은 1보다 크거나 작게 되지."

"당신은 너무 똑똑해서 섹시할 때가 있어."

영경이 씩 웃었다.

"그래? 너무 간헐적이라 탈이지. 그런데 우리는 어떨까? 1이 될까?"

"모르지."

수환의 말에 영경이 중얼거렸다.

"내 병은 내 분모의 크기를 얼마나 측량할 수 없이 크게 하고 있을까?"

"그렇지 않아. 당신은 아직도 분모보다 분자가 훨씬 더 큰 사람이야."

"과연 그럴까?"

영경이 쓸쓸하게 웃었다.

"과연 그래."

"근데 환아, 나는 사람들이 내 병을 병으로 보지 않는다는 느낌이 들어. 의사들까지도 그런 것 같아. 그럴 때면 심하게 위축돼. 당신은 어때? 1이 될 것 같아?"

"그건 당신이 정해줘."

"알았어. 다녀와서 정해줄게."

"그래, 그렇게 해."

gyeong tried to take off her glasses with the other. Her hand was shaking, as she almost, but not quite, touched her glasses. After she had suffered from spasms a few days ago, Yeong-gyeong's hands were still shaky.

Finally snatching her glasses off, Yeong-gyeong said, "I thought about this metaphor and it seems like you can apply it to everyone. If we think of someone's strong points as the numerator and their shortcomings as the denominator, we can find the value of that person. No matter how great a person's strength is, if his shortcomings are greater than his strengths, then, their value is less than 1, and vice versa."

"So, 1 is the standard," said Su-hwan.

"That's right. Everyone is either bigger or smaller than 1."

"You're sometimes so smart you're sexy."

Yeong-gyeong smiled and said, "Yeah? Problem is that it's not very often. Anyway, what do you think our values are? Can we get to 1?"

"I don't know," said Su-hwan.

Yeong-gyeong murmured, "How immeasurably does my illness enhance the size of my denominator?"

수환은 이렇게 말했지만, 실은 자신의 병이야말로 분모를 무한대로 늘리고 있어서 자신의 값은 1보다 작은 건 물론이고 점점 0에 수렴되어가고 있는 중이라고 생각하고 있었다. 아니, 꼭 병 때문만은 아닐지도 몰랐다. 그는 마흔세 살에 영경을 만난 후로 취한 영경을 집까지 업어오는 일 말고 영경에게 해준 것이 거의 없었다. 그러니 분모가 이토록 확 늘어나기 전에도 이미 분자의 숫자마저 미미했던 것이다. 그러나 지금 그런 말을 영경에게 하는 건 좋지 않을 것 같았다. 영경이 기꺼운 마음으로 외출할 수 있게 해주는 게 그나마 자신의 분자를 조금이라도 늘리는 일이라고, 영경에게서 자신의 존재감을 조금이라도 크게 하는 일이라고 수환은 생각했다.

수환은 스무 살에 쇳일을 시작해 10년 넘게 선반 절단 용접 제관 등 쇠 다루는 모든 기술을 익혔다. 서른셋에 친구와 작은 규모의 철공소를 차려 공업사 수준으로 키워내는 데 성공했다. 한때 공장이 쌩쌩 돌아갈 적엔 제법 돈을 벌기도 했지만 거래처의 횡포로 갑작스레 판로가 막히는 바람에 부도를 맞았다. 위장이혼을 제안한

"That's not right. Your numerator is much larger than your denominator," Su-hwan said.

"Is it, really?" Yeong-gyeong smiled sadly.

"It is, really."

"But, Hwan, I feel like people don't consider my illness an illness. Even doctors. When I think that, I get extremely depressed. How about you? Do you think you'll be a 1?"

"You tell me."

"Okay. I'll tell you after I come back."

"Yes, do."

Although Su-hwan spoke like this, he thought that since his illness was extending his denominator to infinity, his value was not only smaller than 1, but also approaching zero. No, it was not even just his illness. Since he had met Yeong-gyeong at the age of forty-three, he hadn't done anything much for Yeong-gyeong other than piggyback her when she was drunk. Therefore, even before his denominator had begun expanding like this, the value of his numerator had become quite insignificant. But he felt it wise not to say such a thing to Yeong-gyeong now. Su-hwan thought that helping Yeong-gyeong go out now would be a way to increase his numerator, a way to make his value ever

아내는 이혼하자마자 자기 명의로 변경된 집과 재산을 모조리 팔아 잠적해버렸다. 듣기로는 외국에 나갔다고 했지만 알 수 없는 일이었다. 다행히 자식은 없었다. 서른아홉에 신용불량자가 된 그는 지금껏 변변한 돈벌이를 해본 적이 없었다. 단순영업직, 택배, 대리운전 등 닥치는 대로 일을 했지만 한동안은 일을 놓고 공황상태에 빠진 적도 있었고 한 달 정도 노숙생활을 한 적도 있었다. 이후로 알음알음 선배나 친구가 하는 사업을 도와주며 생계를 유지했다. 친구의 재혼식에서 영경을 만나기 전까지 수환은 언제든 자살할 수 있다는 생각을 단검처럼 지니고 살았다. 그날이 무뎌지지 않도록 밤마다 자살할 시기를 저울질하며 마음을 벼리는 힘으로 하루하루를 버텼다.

영경은 스물세 살에 중등교사임용을 받아 국어교사로 20년을 재직한 후 마흔셋에 퇴직했다. 서른둘에 결혼을 했고 1년 반 만에 이혼했다. 전남편은 이혼하자마자 다른 여자와 재혼했다. 그는 자기 부모의 반대를 무릅쓰고 백일 된 아들의 양육을 영경이 맡는 데 동의했다. 다만 한 달에 한 번씩 자기 부모에게 아이를 하루 정도 맡길 것을 요구했고 영경도 거기에 합의했다. 아이

so much bigger.

Su-hwan began ironwork when he was twenty and had practiced all the ironwork techniques such as lathing, cutting, welding, and boiler manufacturing for over ten years. When he was thirty-three, he set up a small iron foundry with his friend and successfully grew it to a mid-sized factory. He made some money when the factory was running in full force, but had to file for bankruptcy when a major customer made unreasonable demands and he could not find any other customers. His wife proposed that they divorced to protect their assets, but ran away as soon as their divorce went through. She had sold off their house and all their assets. They said that she had gone abroad, but he did not know whether that rumor was true or not. Fortunately, they hadn't had any children. With his credit bad since thirty-nine, he couldn't get a decent job. He worked at random as a store clerk, deliveryman, and proxy driver. For a while, he could not work at all, depressed and panicked. He lived as a homeless man for about a month. Since then, he made his living by helping friends and acquaintances with their businesses. Until Su-hwan

가 돌을 앞두고 있던 어느 날 아이를 데려간 예전 시부모로부터 앞으로는 자기들이 손자를 키울 테니 걱정하지 말라는 연락이 왔다. 전남편 부부와 예전 시부모는 그녀 모르게 은밀히 준비해 아이를 데리고 이민을 떠나버렸다. 경찰에 납치신고를 내고 소송을 준비하는 영경에게, 영선은 그럴 것 없다고, 차라리 잘 된 일이니 내버려두라고 했고 영미는 울면서 하나님께 기도하자고 했다. 그때부터 영경은 언니들과 오랫동안 만나지 않았고, 모든 일에서 손을 놓고 술을 마시기 시작했다. 점점 알코올의존증이 깊어져 지각이 잦고 학교 일에 태만해졌다. 더 이상 교사로서의 업무를 감당하지 못하고 있다는 죄책감과 걷잡을 수 없이 나빠진 평판 때문에 그녀는 미흔셋에 퇴직을 결심했다. 퇴직한 지 두어 달쯤 지나 친구의 재혼식에서 수환을 만났을 때 영경은 술을 마시면서 자꾸 가까이 앉은 수환의 눈을 들여다보았다. 그리고 그가 조용히 등을 내밀어 그녀를 업었을 때 그녀는 취한 와중에도 자신에게 돌아올 행운의 몫이 아직 남아있었다는 사실에 놀라고 의아해했다.

요양원은 본관 건물과 별채 건물 두 동으로 이루어져

met Yeong-gyeong at his friend's wedding, he had lived thinking that he could kill himself without any consequences anytime he wanted. This thought was like a dagger he kept on himself at all times. He could manage to get by each day with the strength he generated by reforging that blade and considering the right time to commit suicide every night.

Since she had been employed at twenty-three, Yeong-gyeong taught Korean for twenty years until she reached the age of forty-three. She married when she was thirty-two and got divorced within that year. Her ex-husband remarried as soon as they were divorced. Despite his parents' objections, he agreed to grant Yeong-gyeong custody of their three-month old son. He asked Yeong-gyeong to bring their son to his parents one day every month and Yeong-gyeong agreed. One day, a little before the baby's first birthday, Yeong-gyeong's ex-in-laws, who had taken their grandson for the day, called and informed Yeong-gyeong that they would raise the baby from then on and that she needed not worry about it anymore. It turned out that her ex-husband and his parents emigrated with the baby after secretly

있었다. 웅장하고 규모가 큰 본관 건물에는 입원병실과 언제 입원할지 모르는 중증환자들의 숙소가 있었고, 펜션처럼 보이는 별채 두 동에는 요양원 직원과 일반요양인 들의 숙소와 휴게실, 운동시설 등이 있었다. 널찍한 주차장 한편에는 응급환자들을 수송하기 위한 앰뷸런스 두 대가 주차되어 있고, 정문 쪽으로는 아담한 정원이, 본관 건물을 감싼 뒷산 쪽으로는 조경이 잘 된 산책로가 있었다.

젊은 청년이 수환의 휠체어를 밀고와 본관 현관에 세워놓은 후 영경에게 말했다.

"자리 비켜줄게요, 아줌마."

"고맙다, 종우야."

종우는 영경이 외출할 때마다 수환을 돌봐주는 단골 간병인이었다. 청년이 멀찍이 가기도 전에 영경이 허리를 구부려 수환에게 입 맞추려 하자 수환이 고개를 돌렸다.

"뭐야? 마음이 식은 거야?"

영경이 장난스럽게 물었다.

"아니, 입냄새 때문에 그래."

수환이 입을 가리며 말했다.

plotting to take him. While Yeong-gyeong went to the police with the kidnapping charge and was preparing for a lawsuit, Yeong-seon told her to leave it alone, saying that it was all for the better, and Yeong-mi, sobbing, told her to pray to God. Since then, Yeong-gyeong had not seen her sisters for a long time. She also began to drink, unable to focus on anything else. As she became more and more dependent on alcohol, she became frequently late for school and careless in her work. Feeling guilty for not fully fulfilling her duties as a teacher and because of her worsening reputation, Yeong-gyeong decided to retire at forty-three. When she met Su-hwan at her friend's wedding about two or three months after her retirement, Yeong-gyeong had stared steadily into the eyes of Su-hwan, who had been sitting nearby. When he silently offered his back towards her and piggybacked her home, she was surprised, even in her drunkenness, that she still had the good fortune to receive even this. It was hard for her to believe it.

The nursing home was composed of three buildings—the main building and the two annex buildings. The grand and large main building housed in-

"그게 뭐 어때서? 입이 말라서 그런 건데."

"그래도 오늘따라 유난히 짜고 쓰네."

"난 괜찮아."

"내가 싫어. 달콤까지는 안 돼도 간간한 정도만이라도 지키고 싶어서 그래."

"참 까탈스럽게 군다. 내 입에서 술냄새 나면 당신 근처에도 못 가겠다."

"그런 거 아니야."

"뭐가 아니야?"

"아직도 내가 우리 빵경이한테 잘 보이고 싶나보지. 당신 들어올 때까진 어떻게든 간간한 정도로 낮춰놓을게."

"그럼 당신이 해줘."

영경이 쑥 파인 볼을 내밀었다. 수환은 숨을 멈추고 가만히 영경의 볼에 입술을 갖다댔다.

"다녀올게."

"그래. 잘 다녀와."

수환은 허깨비같이 걸어가는 영경의 깡마른 뒷모습을 보면서 그녀가 돌아올 때까지 자신이 과연 버틸 수 있을지, 그리고 그녀가 무사히 돌아올 수 있을지를 생

patient ward and rooms for patients with serious conditions in imminent danger of hospitalization. In the two annex buildings that looked like homestay lodgings, there were units for the nursing home staff and for the nursing home residents with less serious conditions, a lounge, and a gym. Two ambulances for emergency patients were parked at a corner of a large parking lot. There was a pretty garden near the main gate and a nicely landscaped walkway towards a hill behind the main building. The hill looked as if it was embracing the building from behind.

A young man parked Su-hwan's wheelchair that he had pushed near the entryway of the main building and said to Yeong-gyeong, "Take your time. I'll be over there."

"Thank you, Jong-u."

Jong-u was a regular caretaker who took care of Su-hwan whenever Yeong-gyeong went out on leave. Even before the young man had gone far, Yeong-gyeong bent over to kiss Su-hwan, who turned his head away.

"What? You don't love me anymore?" Yeong-gyeong asked playfully.

"No. It's because of the smell in my mouth," Su-

각했다. 언제나 영경이 외출할 때마다 드는 생각이었다. 영경은 이틀 만에 돌아오겠다고 했지만 요 근래엔 이틀 만에 돌아온 적이 거의 없었다. 사흘도 아니고, 나흘도 아니고, 지난번엔 일주일 만에 거의 송장 꼴이 되어 돌아왔었다. 수환은 어쩌면 이게 정말 마지막일지 모른다는 생각을 했지만 합병증인 쇼그렌증후군으로 림프선이 말라붙어 눈물은 나지 않았다.

종우가 다가와 휠체어 손잡이를 잡으며 물었다.

"들어갈래요, 아저씨?"

"조금만 더 있다 들어가자."

"그래요."

수환은 종우에게서 풍기는 옅은 담배냄새를 맡았다. 동네병원에서 류마티스 진단을 받고 곧바로 담배를 끊었으니 끊은 지 2년이 넘었다. 끊기 전까지는 그야말로 골초였다. 문득 담배가 피우고 싶다는 생각이 들었다.

"산책 좀 할래요?"

종우가 물었다.

"아니야. 그냥 여기 있을란다."

"힘들죠, 아저씨?"

"아직 괜찮다."

hwan said, covering his mouth.

"What about it? It's because your mouth gets dry."

"Still, it feels especially salty and bitter today."

"I don't care."

"I don't like it. I want to keep it moderately salty even if it can't be sweet."

"How fussy! I shouldn't go near you when I smell like alcohol, then."

"That's not it."

"What's not it?"

"I guess I would still like to look decent to Bbang-gyeong. I'll make it less salty until you come back."

"You kiss me, then."

Yeong-gyeong offered her gaunt cheek to Su-hwan. Su-hwan held his breath and touched Yeong-gyeong's cheek lightly with his lips.

"I'll be back soon."

"Okay. Take care."

Looking at Yeong-gyeong's skinny back as she walked away like a ghost, Su-hwan wondered if he could survive until she returned, and if Yeong-gyeong could come back safe and sound. That's what was always on his mind whenever Yeong-gyeong left. Although Yeong-gyeong always said

"그러니까 뭐하러 그 독한 주사까지 맞고 멀쩡한 척 해요?"

청년이 툴툴거렸다.

"안 그러면 못 가, 저 사람."

"못 가면 더 좋죠. 담당선생님도 아까 막 뭐라 하시던데."

"종우야."

"네."

"여자친구한테 선물해본 적 있냐?"

"있죠. 아, 나는 여자애들 선물 고르는 게 제일 싫어요."

"그게 왜 싫어?"

"뭘 해줘야 할지 모르겠잖아요. 근데 선물이 왜요?"

"아니야. 그냥 물어봤어."

잠시 뒤 종우가 말했다.

"이거 선물 아니에요, 아저씨. 이렇게 자꾸 나가는 거 아줌마한테도 안 좋은 일이잖아요?"

"분모야 어쩔 수 없다 쳐도 분자라도 늘려야지."

"네? 부모가 뭐요?"

"아니다, 아무것도."

that she would come back in two days, she rarely did these days. Last time, it wasn't until after three or four days, but a week until she had come back. She had looked like a corpse then. Although Su-hwan thought this might be the last time he saw her, he couldn't cry because his lymphatic glands had dried up due to Sjogren's syndrome, one of the complications of his illness.

Jong-u approached him and grasped the wheel-chair handles, asking, "Do you want to go back to your room, Uncle?"

"Just a little later."

"Okay."

Su-hwan could smell the tobacco faintly wafting from Jong-u. Su-hwan had quit smoking more than two years ago, immediately after he was diagnosed with rheumatism at the neighborhood clinic. He used to be a chain smoker before then. Suddenly, he felt like smoking.

"Would you like to go out for a little bit?" Jong-u asked.

"No, I'll stay here."

"It's hard, isn't it, Uncle?"

"It's not too bad as of yet."

"So, why did you get that drug injection and pre-

수환은 처음 영경을 만나던 봄날을 생각했다. 웨딩홀에서 사람들에 섞여 있을 때부터 그는 영경을 주목하고 있었다. 한 달 동안 노숙생활을 했을 때 본 여자 노숙자들을 생각나게 하는 얼굴이었다. 비록 화장을 하고 있었지만 영경의 눈가는 쌍안경 자국처럼 깊게 패였고 볼은 말랑한 주머니처럼 늘어져 있었다. 재혼한 친구의 집에 몰려가 술을 마실 때 그는 영경과 가까운 자리에 앉았다. 술을 마실수록 영경의 얼굴은 붉어지기보다 회색에 가까워졌고 표정은 딱딱하게 굳어 막 마르기 시작하는 석고상처럼 보였다. 가끔 그녀는 취한 눈으로 그의 눈을 빤히 들여다보곤 했다. 취한 그녀를 업었을 때 혹시 달그락거리는 소리가 나지 않을까 염려될 정도로 앙상하고 가벼운 뼈만을 가진 부피감에 놀랐던 기억이 있다. 그 봄밤이 시작이었고 이 봄밤이 마지막일지 몰랐다.

수환은 진통제 기운이 떨어질 때까지 영경이 마지막으로 사라진 지점을 바라보고 있었다.

막차를 타고 읍내에 내린 영경은 편의점에 들어가 맥주 두 캔과 소주 한 병을 샀다. 편의점 스탠드에 서서 맥

tend that you were fine?" grumbled the young man.

"If I didn't, she couldn't have gone out."

"All the better for that, then! Her doctor was nagging her, too."

"Jong-u!"

"Yes."

"Have you given a gift to your girlfriend?"

"Yeah. Oh, I hate picking gifts for girls so much!"

"Why do you hate it?"

"I don't know what to get. But, why are you bringing up gifts?"

"No reason. I just asked."

A little later, Jong-u said, "That wasn't a gift for her, Uncle. It's not good for her to leave so often, is it?"

"If there's nothing I can do about my denominator, then I should at least increase the value of my numerator."

"What? What are you talking about?"

"Nothing. It's nothing."

Su-hwan thought of the spring day when he had first met Yeong-gyeong. He had taken notice of her at the wedding hall, even when she was in the middle of other people. Her face reminded him of the homeless women he had run into when he

주 한 캔을 따서 한 모금 마신 후 캔의 좁은 입구에 소주를 따랐다. 또 한 모금 마시고 소주를 따랐다. 그런 식으로 맥주 두 캔과 소주 한 병을 비우는 데 30분도 걸리지 않았다. 몸은 오슬오슬 떨렸지만 속은 후끈후끈 달아올랐다. 꽉 조였던 나사가 돌돌 풀리면서 유쾌하고 나른한 생명감이 충만해졌다. 이게 모두 중독된 몸이 일으키는 거짓된 반응이라는 걸 알고 있었지만 그까짓 것은 아무래도 좋았다. 젖을 빠는 허기진 아이처럼 그녀의 몸은 더 많은 알코올을 쭉쭉 흡수하기를 원했다.

영경은 컵라면과 소주 한 병을 샀다. 컵라면에 물을 부으며 그녀는 이제 시작일 뿐이라고, 서둘지 말자고 스스로에게 타일렀다. 애타도록 마음에 서둘지 말라. 영경은 작게 읊조렸다. 강물 위에 떨어진 불빛처럼 혁혁한 업적을 바라지 말라. 개가 울고 종이 울리고 달이 떠도 너는 조금도 당황하지 말라. 영경은 자신의 중얼거리는 목소리가 점점 커지는 것을 알지 못했다. 계속 뭐라고 중얼거리며 소주와 컵라면을 먹는 그녀를 사람들이 곁눈질했다.

영경은 컵라면과 소주 한 병을 비우고 과자 한 봉지와 페트 소주와 생수를 사가지고 편의점을 나왔다. 눈

lived as a homeless man for a month. Although she had put on make-up, there were deep dark circles around her eyes like the traces of a binocular and her cheeks were drooping like soft pouches. When they went to the married couple's house to drink, he had taken a seat near Yeong-gyeong. The more Yeong-gyeong drank, the closer to gray her face became rather than red. Her facial expression became so hardened that it looked like a plaster sculpture just beginning to dry. Her eyes drunk, she occasionally stared at his eyes. He remembered how surprised he was at the lightness of her body when he had piggybacked her home. She was so skinny and bony that he thought that she might make a clattering sound. That spring night was the beginning, and this spring night could be the end.

Su-hwan was staring at the spot from which Yeong-gyeong disappeared last.

When Yeong-gyeong got off at the downtown station from the last bus, she went straight to a convenience store and bought two cans of beer and a bottle of *soju*. As she stood at the convenience store counter, she opened a can of beer,

을 뜨지 않은 땅속의 벌레같이! 영경은 큰소리로 외치며 걸었다. 아둔하고 가난한 마음은 서둘지 말라! 애타도록 마음에 서둘지 말라! 영경은 작은 모텔 입구에 멈춰 섰다. 절제여! 나의 귀여운 아들이여! 오오 나의 영감이여! 갑자기 수환이 보고 싶었다. 오후에 면회를 온 영선과 영미 생각도 났다. 그 아이가 살아있다면, 하고 생각하다 영경은 고개를 흔들었다. 촛불 모양의 흰 봉오리를 매단 목련나무 아래에서 그녀는 소리 내어 울었다. 울면서도 자신이 슬퍼서 우는 게 아니라 감정조절장애 때문에 우는 것이라고 생각했다. 의사는 그녀의 모든 신체적 감정적 반응들이 거짓이라고 했다. 그럴지도 모른다고 그녀는 생각했다. 모텔 방에 들어가자마자 수환에게 전화를 하고 언니들에게도 전화를 해야겠다고 생각했다. 딱 오늘 하룻밤만 마시고 요양원으로 돌아가야겠다고 생각했다. 그녀는 그렇게 할 수 있고 마땅히 그렇게 할 것이었다. 성마른 몸에 취한 피가 돌면서 그녀의 눈에 모든 것이 아주 단순하고 명료해 보였다. 손도 떨리지 않고 금세라도 깊이 잠들 수 있을 것 같았다. 영경은 모텔 현관 계단을 올라가며 시의 마지막 부분을 또박또박 반복했다.

took a sip, and poured *soju* into the small opening of the beer can. She drank another sip and poured more *soju* into her can again. It took her less than thirty minutes to empty two cans of beer and a bottle of *soju* in this way. Although she felt it was chilly outside, she thought it felt red-hot inside of herself. She felt she was filled with a sense of a pleasant and languid vitality, as if tight screws had been loosened from her body. She knew that this was all a false response of a body addicted to alcohol, but she did not care. Her body wanted to absorb even more alcohol, like a hungry baby sucking at her mother's breast.

Yeong-gyeong bought a cup ramen and a bottle of *soju*. She poured water into the ramen cup and told herself that this was just a beginning, that she shouldn't hurry. *Don't be anxious, don't hurry*, Yeong-gyeong softly recited. *Don't wish for an achievement as brilliant as lights reflected on the river. Don't get disconcerted at all even if the dog barks, the bell rings, and the moon rises*. Yeong-gyeong was not aware that her voice was growing louder. People were glancing at her muttering, eating ramen, and drinking *soju*.

After finishing the cup ramen and the bottle of *soju*, Yeong-gyeong bought a bag of snacks, a

절. 제. 여. 나. 의. 귀. 여. 운. 아. 들. 이. 여. 오. 오. 나. 의. 영. 감. 이. 여.*

종우는 간병인으로서 자기가 할 수 있는 일이 아무것도 없다는 걸 알았다. 의사들의 최종 처치도 끝났다. 이마와 가슴과 양 옆구리에 냉팩을 빈틈없이 끼워 놓았지만 수환의 열은 가라앉지 않았다.

"아저씨, 내 얘기 들려요?"

수환은 말없이 숨을 헐떡거렸다.

"아줌마는 연락이 안 되고요, 이제 아저씨네 엄마랑 형이 온댔어요. 그때까진 기다릴 수 있죠?"

종우는 가망이 없는 줄 알면서도 30분마다 한 번씩 영경의 꺼진 휴대폰으로 전화를 걸어보았다. 서울에서 출발한 수환의 가족이 언제 도착할지는 확실하지 않았다. 세 시간 또는 네 시간 뒤?

아침 햇살이 쏟아져 들어와 병실이 환했지만 종우는 왠지 무서운 생각이 들었다. 간병인이 된 후로 그는 아직까지 누군가의 죽음을 혼자 맞이해본 적이 없었다. 많건 적건 늘 환자의 곁에는 가족들이 있었다.

"내가 얘기 하나 해줄까요?"

large plastic bottle of *soju*, and a bottle of water and left the convenience store. *Like a worm with its eyes closed under the soil!* Yeong-gyeong walked, shouting out loud. *Don't hurry, you, you poor, stupid soul! Don't be anxious, don't hurry!* Yeong-gyeong stopped in front of a small motel. *Self-restraint! My dear child! Oh, oh, my inspiration!* Suddenly she missed Su-hwan. She thought of Yeong-seon and Yeong-mi who had visited her in the afternoon. Yeong-gyeong thought, *if the baby was alive*, and then shook her head. She stood under a magnolia tree, its white buds like candles, and began to sob loudly. She thought that she was crying not because she was sad, but because of her impulse control disorder. Her doctor told her that all her physical and emotional responses were false. She thought that his diagnosis might be true. She decided that she should call Su-hwan and her elder sisters as soon as she entered the motel room. She thought that she should go back to the nursing home after just one night of drinking. She could do it and she should. She could feel her blood circulating through her impatient body, everything seemed simple and clear to her. Her hands weren't shaking, and she felt like falling asleep immediately.

종우는 죽어가는 사람에게 최후로 남아 있는 감각이 청각이라는 얘기를 들은 기억이 나서 이렇게 말했다. 그런데 막상 무슨 얘기를 해야 좋을지 몰랐다.

"여기 사람들이 아저씨랑 아줌마 보고 뭐라는지 알아요? 이산가족 같대요. 맨날 아침마다 두 사람 만날 때면 이산가족 만나는 것 같대요. 난 아줌마 별로 안 좋아하는데 어쩔 때 아줌마가 아저씨 빤히 쳐다볼 때는 괜히 눈물 나요. 아, 참, 며칠 전에 아저씨가 선물 얘기 했잖아요? 여자친구한테 주는 선물이요."

종우는 심박측정기의 그래프를 바라보며 생각에 잠겼다. 왜 갑자기 그 애 얼굴이 떠올랐는지 모를 일이었다.

"여자애들은 선물 받는 거 진짜 좋아해요. 어떨 땐 대놓고 뻔뻔하게 요구해요. 근데 진짜 선물 사달라는 말을 한 번도 안 한 여자애가 있었어요."

종우는 힐긋 수환을 보았다. 수환은 여전히 고열에 시달리고 있었다. 담당의 말로는 주기적으로 오르내리는 열의 수준이 아니라고 했다.

"아, 혼자 얘기하려니 답답하네."

종우는 목소리를 높였다.

"아저씨, 그러니까 내가요, 학교 때 운동 좀 했다고 얘

As she climbed up the stairs at the entrance of the motel, Yeong-gyeong recited the last part of the poem:

SELF-RESTRAINT! MY DEAR CHILD! OH, OH, MY INSPIRATION!

Jong-u realized that there was nothing he could do as a caretaker. The doctors had finished their last treatments. Although they had put icepacks all over Su-hwan's body—over his forehead, on his chest, and beside both of his sides—, Su-hwan remained feverish.

"Uncle, can you hear me?"

Su-hwan gasped softly.

"We cannot reach your wife. Your mother and brother are on their way. You can wait for them, can't you?"

Jong-u called Yeong-gyeong's cell phone every thirty minutes, although he knew it was of no use, because her phone was turned off. It was unclear when Su-hwan's family would arrive from Seoul. Perhaps three or four hours later?

The hospital room was bright with the morning sunrays pouring in. Jong-u felt scared for some reason. He had never faced a patient's death alone

기했죠? 역도는 진짜 잘해가지고 아마 대회 같은 데 나가서 입상도 하고 그랬어요. 그러다가 언제부터 암벽등반에 빠지게 됐는데 그게 무지하게 재밌더라고요. 거기 동호회에서 여자애들도 만나고 그랬는데 내가 처음엔 딴 애를 좋아했거든요. 근데 그 딴 애랑 그 애가 친한 것 같더라고요. 그래서 그 애한테 접근해가지고 장난도 걸고, 뭐 좋아하냐, 선물 받고 싶은 거 없냐, 물어보기도 하고 그랬는데, 그 애가 그런 거 없다고 하더라고요. 그래서 그냥 그런가보다 하고 말았어요. 나는 쭉 딴 애한테 마음이 가 있던 거니까."

종우는 갑자기 말을 끊고 자리에서 벌떡 일어나 창가로 가서 본관 뒤뜰을 내려다보았다. 잠시 뒤에 그는 수환 쪽으로 몸을 돌렸다.

"나 담배 한 대 피우고 들어와도 돼요, 아저씨?"

열에 들떠 위로 올라가 있는 수환의 검은 동자가 좌우로 살짝 흔들리는 것 같았다.

"알았어요, 아저씨."

종우는 체념한 얼굴로 돌아와 자리에 앉았다.

"얘기를 계속하면요, 그 딴 애가 갑자기 나한테 관심을 보이기 시작한 거예요. 내가 자기를 안 좋아하고 그

since he had become a caretaker. There were always family members next to the patients, either a lot or a few.

"Shall I tell you a story?" Jong-u asked, remembering that one's hearing was the last sense to go from a dying patient. But, he did not know what to tell Su-hwan.

"Do you know what other people say about you and your wife? They say that you're like a reunited family. Whenever you two see each other every morning, you look like family meeting each other for the first time after a long separation. I don't like your wife much, but I feel like crying for no reason when your wife stares at you sometimes. Oh, wait, you talked about getting a gift a few days ago, right? A gift for a girlfriend."

Jong-u fell into a deep thought, looking at the electrocardiogram graph. He was not sure why he suddenly remembered that girl's face.

"Girls really like to get gifts. Sometimes, they even shamelessly demand them. But I knew a girl who never said anything like that."

Jong-u glanced at Su-hwan quickly. Su-hwan was still feverish. According to his doctor, this was not the regular periodic cycle of fever.

애를 좋아하는 줄 안 거죠. 근데 왜 그랬는지 모르겠는데 내가 그렇다고 해버렸어요. 그래 나 소연이 좋아한다 어쩔래, 그런 거죠. 그러고 나니까 웃긴 게 얘가 은근히 달라붙더라고요. 여기서 얘는 소연이가 아니고 딴 애, 은경이 말이에요. 아, 씨, 내가 왜 이런 얘길 하고 있지?"

종우는 손을 우둑거리며 잠시 멍한 상태로 앉아 있었다. 열린 문틈으로 늙은 간호사가 지나가는 게 보였다. 요양원 사람들은 입주자들뿐 아니라 의사와 간호사, 직원들까지도 모두 늙었다. 힘을 써야 하는 몇몇 간병인들만이 젊었다. 종우는 자신이 언제까지 이곳에 있을 수 있을까 생각했다.

"그러니까 내가 그때 바로 은경이랑 사귀었으면 됐을 건데, 왜 그랬는지 모르겠는데 계속 소연이한테 잘해주고 좋아하는 척하고 그런 거예요. 은경이가 몸이 달아서 어쩔 줄 몰라 하는 게 재밌었던 거죠. 소연이 생각은 하나도 안 하고. 진짜 안 했어요, 그 애 생각은. 나 못됐죠?"

종우는 문득 생각난 듯 휴대폰을 꺼내 전화를 걸었다.

"이 아줌마 진짜 못됐다."

그리고 수환을 힐긋 보고 고개를 끄덕였다.

"알았어요, 알았어. 아줌마 욕 안 할게요. 근데 이상한

"Oh, it's hard to talk to myself." Jong-u raised her voice and said, "Uncle, so, didn't I tell you that I was quite the athlete in school? I was really good at weight lifting—so good that I won some medals at competitions. But, at some point, I fell in love with rock climbing. There were girls at the rock-climbing club. At first, I liked another girl, who it seemed was a very close friend to the girl I'm talking about. So I approached this girl and tried to flirt with her. I asked her if she wanted a gift, what she liked. But she said that she did not want anything. So, I thought, okay. I was interested in another girl, anyway." Jong-u suddenly stopped talking. He stood up abruptly, went to the window, and looked down at the backyard of the main building.

"May I come back after smoking a cigarette, Uncle?" The black pupils in Su-hwan's feverish eyes looked upwards and seemed to flit left and right slightly.

"Okay, Uncle." Jong-u came back with a resigned look on his face and sat back down on his chair.

"So, if I may continue, that other girl suddenly began to show interest in me. She thought that I liked her friend, not her. And, I don't know why, but I told her that I did. *I like So-yeon, so?* That's

거 하나 있어요. 내가 왜 이런 얘길 하냐 하면요, 아줌마 우는 거 보면 자꾸 소연이 생각이 나요."

종우는 심박측정기에서 나는 기계음에 귀를 기울이며 누군가 지금 자기 곁에 있어주었으면 좋겠다고 생각했다. 그게 소연이었으면 어떨까 하고도 생각했다.

"내가 은경이랑 사귀기로 하고 소연이한테 헤어지자고 얘기했을 때, 와, 나 진짜 쫄았거든요. 소연이 걔가 막 울고불고 할 줄 알았는데 전혀 울지를 않더라고요. 눈은 막 울 것 같은데 끝까지 울지를 않더라고요. 그냥 알았다고, 헤어지자고 그러는데 혹시 얘가 그동안 내 마음을 다 알고 있었나 싶어서 겁나기도 하고 또 징징거리지 않아서 잘 됐다 싶기도 하고, 암튼 이상했어요. 집에 간다길래 택시 잡아주려고 서 있는데 갑자기 얘가 코피를 쏟는 거예요. 난 세상에 그렇게 무섭게 코피 쏟는 거는 처음 봤어요. 그 밤중에, 아무 짓도 안 했는데 코피가 그냥……"

종우는 말을 멈췄다. 수환의 숨소리가 급격히 가빠졌다 가라앉았다.

"코피가 그냥……"

수환의 목에서 꺼억 하는 소리가 났다.

what I said. Funnily, after that, she began quietly clinging to me. I mean, Eun-gyeong, not So-yeon. Oh, jeez, why am I talking about this?" Jong-u snapped his fingers loudly and sat staring blankly ahead for a while. He saw an old nurse pass by through the open door. The people in the nursing home were all old, not only the patients, but also the doctors, nurses, and other staff members. Only a few caretakers whose work demanded physical strength were young. Jong-u wondered how long he would remain here.

"So, I should have dated Eun-gyeong then and there, but, God only knows why, I pretended that I liked So-yeon, paying most of my attention to her. I enjoyed seeing Eun-gyeong become fretful and anxious. I wasn't thinking of So-yeon. I really wasn't. What an awful kid I was!"

Suddenly remembering something, Jong-u took out his cell phone and began to dial.

"A really awful woman she is!"

Then, he glanced at Su-hwan and nodded.

"Okay, okay. I won't speak ill of her. But, there's something strange. The reason why I tell you this story is... When I see your wife cry, I am very often reminded of So-yeon." Jong-u listened to the me-

"코피가……"

심박측정기의 그래프가 일직선으로 내려앉으며 기계음이 길게 울렸다.

"아저씨."

종우는 몇 초 동안 기다렸다.

"아저씨, 이러지 마!"

종우가 빽 소리치며 비상벨을 눌렀다.

"아줌마는 어쩔 거야, 이제?"

모텔 주인의 신고로 의식불명인 영경이 요양원의 앰뷸런스에 실려 왔을 때는 수환의 장례가 다 끝난 후였다. 영경은 이틀 만에 의식을 되찾았지만 온전히 되찾은 것은 아니었다. 영경은 수환에 대해 묻지 않았다. 직원들도 수환에 대해 말하지 않았다. 담당의가 영경을 상담한 후 화난 얼굴로 전화를 거는 것을 간호사 몇 명이 보았다. 다음날 영선과 영미가 요양원으로 찾아왔지만 영경은 그들조차 알아보지 못했다. 법적 대리인이자 보호자가 된 영선과 영미의 동의로 영경은 알코올성 치매로 인한 금치산 상태에 놓였다. 그 이후로 영경은 잦은 경련과 발작 등 지독한 금단증상에 시달렸지만 다행

chanical sound of the electrocardiogram and thought it would be better if someone was with him then. He thought how it would be if that person were So-yeon.

"When I decided to date Eun-gyeong and told So-yeon that I wanted to break up with her, I was really worried. I thought So-yeon would make a fuss, cry and what not; but she didn't cry at all. Although her eyes looked like they were about to tear up, she didn't show any tears at all until we parted. She just said, *Okay, let's break up*. I was kind of scared, wondering if she knew my feelings all along. I also felt relieved that she didn't throw a tantrum. Anyway, it was a strange feeling. She said she wanted to go home, so I stood with her to hail a taxi for her until suddenly she had a nosebleed. Goodness, I had never seen someone bleed so much from her nose. At night. For no reason, blood just came pouring out of her nose..."

Jong-u stopped. Su-hwan's breathing suddenly quickened and then slowed down.

"Blood just poured..."

Su-hwan gasped.

"Blood..."

With a long mechanical sound, the electrocar-

히 그녀의 몸은 어려운 고비를 잘 견뎌냈다.

몸이 어느 정도 회복된 후에도 영경은 여전히 수환의 존재를 기억해내지 못했다. 다만 자신의 인생에서 뭔가 엄청난 것이 증발되었다는 것만은 느끼고 있는 듯했다. 영경은 계속 뭔가를 찾아 두리번거렸고 다른 환자들의 병실 문을 함부로 열고 돌아다녔다. 요양원 사람들은 수환이 죽었을 때 자신들이 연락두절인 영경에게 품었던 단단한 적의가 푹 곯인 무처럼 물러져 깊은 동정과 연민으로 바뀐 것을 느꼈다. 영경의 온전치 못한 정신이 수환을 보낼 때까지 죽을힘을 다해 견뎠다는 것을, 그리고 수환이 떠난 후에야 비로소 안심하고 죽어버렸다는 것을, 늙은 그들은 본능적으로 알았다.

가끔 영경의 눈잎엔 조숙한 소녀 같기도 하고 쫓기는 짐승 같기도 한, 놀란 듯하면서도 긴장된 두 개의 눈동자가 떠오르곤 했는데, 그럴 때면 종우가 대체 무슨 일이냐고, 왜 그러느냐고 거듭 묻는데도 영경은 오랜 시간 울기만 했다.

* 김수영의 『봄밤』 중에서.

《문학과사회》, 문학과지성사, 2013 여름호

diogram dropped to a straight line.

"Uncle."

Jong-u waited for a few seconds.

"Uncle, don't!" Jong-u shouted and pressed the emergency button. "What's gonna happen to your wife, now?"

It was after Su-hwan's funeral ended when Yeong-gyeong was finally carried unconscious into the nursing home in an ambulance after a motel owner had called the police. Yeong-gyeong regained consciousness after two days, but her recovery was still incomplete. Yeong-gyeong did not ask about Su-hwan. The nursing home staff did not mention Su-hwan, either. A few nurses saw Yeong-gyeong's doctor make a call, his expression livid, after talking with Yeong-gyeong. The next day, Yeong-seon and Yeong-mi visited the nursing home, but Yeong-gyeong did not recognize them. Yeong-seon and Yeong-mi, her legal guardians and authorized agents, agreed that Yeong-gyeong should be declared legally incompetent due to her alcoholic dementia. Since then, Yeong-gyeong suffered often from spasms and fits, but luckily, her body endured these troubles well.

Even after Yeong-gyeong regained a little more of her health, she still remained unable to remember Su-hwan. She just seemed to feel that something of enormous importance had evaporated from her life. Yeong-gyeong would occasionally search the hospital ward's rooms aimlessly. She opened other patients' room doors at random and wandered around the ward. People in the nursing home, who had felt antipathy towards Yeong-gyeong because she couldn't be reached when Su-hwan died, felt their hatred turn into a deep pity and sympathy towards her, their anger softened like a long boiled turnip. The older people instinctively felt that Yeong-gyeong's impaired mind was trying desperately to stay alive until she could send Su-hwan away, and that it would only feel enough relief to die when Su-hwan had left for the other world.

Occasionally, Yeong-gyeong saw two strained eyes that looked like the eyes of a precocious boy or hunted animal. When this happened, Yeong-gyeong would cry for a while without answering any of Jong-u's same questions. What was the matter? Why was she crying?

Translated by Jeon Seung-hee

해설

Afterword

사랑의 플롯, 플롯의 승리

양윤의 (문학평론가)

여기 권여선이 재창조한 늙은 로미오와 줄리엣이 있다. 로미오와 줄리엣 이야기는 모든 비극적인 사랑의 원형 가운데 하나이다. 만남의 불가능성과 그 불가능성을 자신의 운명으로 수락함으로써 마침내 성취되는 역설적인 사랑의 극점에는 둘의 죽음이 놓여 있다. 이들은 다른 세계에 속한 사람들이고 서로가 더 오래 살아 있으면서 상대의 죽음을 확인해야 했으며 죽음으로써 사랑을 완성했던 자들이다. 고전 〈로미오와 줄리엣〉이 보여준 사랑의 숭고함은 이들의 시간 차 죽음을 통해서 명징하게 드러난다. 사랑하는 연인의 죽음을 바라보는 것, 사랑하는 이의 죽음을 지키는 것. 그것은 이중의 사

A Plot of Love, A Triumph of a Plot

Yang Yun-ui (literary critic)

What Kwon Yeo-sun has recreated in her new short story, "Spring Night," is a novel retelling of the classic story of Romeo and Juliet through the story of the old Romeo and old Juliet couple. The story of Romeo and Juliet is one of many archetypal stories of tragic love. At the height of the story's paradoxical love—achieved only when two lovers accept the impossibility of achieving their love as their fate—lies the death of the two lovers. Each of them, belonging to two different worlds, have to survive each other, confirm their lover's deaths, and then finish the cycle of their love with their respective suicides. The sublime quality of love in this

형선고와 다를 바가 없다. 사랑하는 이가 세상을 떠나는 순간, 그 누가 명증한 정신을 지켜낼 수 있을 것인가. 연인의 죽음 앞에서, "아둔하고 가난한 마음"으로 조급해 않으며 "애타도록 마음에 서둘지 말라"(72쪽)라고 외칠 수 있는 자 누구인가. 시인 김수영의 「봄밤」에서 따온 작품의 제목은 춘정을 뜻하는 로맨틱함과 죽음의 그림자가 내비치는 멜랑콜리의 이중성을 잘 드러낸다.

「봄밤」은 매일 이산하는 가족처럼 하루하루가 몰락이자 죽음인 중년 커플의 종말을 다룬다. 로미오와 줄리엣이 사랑의 대가로 죽음을 얻는다면, 「봄밤」의 부부는 이미 지척에 다가와 있는 죽음이라는 최종점에서 때로는 회상의 삶을 살고 때로는 자학의 삶을 살아간다. 이런 플롯은 예징된 서사를 제공한다는 점에서 죽음의 비극성을 한층 고양시킨다.

알코올 중독자 영경과 류머티즘 환자인 수환은 일명 '알루 커플'로 불린다. 몸 상태가 심각하게 악화되자 수환이 먼저 요양원에 들어왔고, 영경이 세간을 정리하고 따라 들어왔다. 둘의 12년간의 동거생활은 서로의 상처를 지켜보는 돌봄의 시간이었다. 수환과 영경은 전혀 다른 세상에서 살다가 친구의 결혼식장에서 처음 만났

classic story reveals itself only through their sequential deaths. They must both witness and watch over one's lover's death—in effect experiencing a kind of double death sentence. Told and retold, we may now find the lovers' responses a bit overly dramatic, tired at the very least. However, it may not be unreasonable to honestly ask how can one maintain a clear mind at the moment of their significant other's death? How does one advise one's own grieving heart for the need for patience, the necessity of slowing down, trying not to worry, letting go? "Spring Night," taken from the Kim Suyeong poem of the same title, aptly conveys these opposing qualities of love, "Spring" evoking notions of romance at its height and "Night" calling to mind the melancholy of death and the relationship's end.

"Spring Night" deals with the tragic end of a middle-aged couple, for whom each passing day means the decline of the other's health and their respective deaths. To them, everyday is like permanently separating from a family member again and again. Whereas Romeo and Juliet pay for their love with their sudden deaths, the couple in "Spring Night" must endure lives of recollection and self-torment near the end of their lives. And with the

다. 둘 모두 첫 결혼에 실패한 상처가 있다. 이십대부터 쇠를 만지는 일을 하던 수환은 운영하던 철공소가 부도를 맞자 전아내의 권유로 위장이혼을 했다가 큰 빚을 떠안고 신용불량자가 되었다. 수환의 전아내는 남은 재산을 처분해서 종적을 감췄다. 국어교사였던 영경은 결혼에 실패한 후 전남편의 식구들이 몰래 아이를 데리고 이민을 가는 바람에 아이와 생이별을 했다. 이후 알코올 중독에 빠진다.

거래처의 횡포, 전아내의 사기와 잠적, 이혼과 도둑맞은 양육권이 둘을 불행의 끝자리로 내몰았지만, 소설의 초점은 그 불행의 조건을 상세히 밝히는 데 있지 않다. 수환이 중병을 얻게 된 것은 신용불량자가 되어서 의료혜택을 받지 못했기 때문이다. 영경이 실직한 알코올 중독자가 된 것은 아이를 빼앗겼기 때문이다. 그럼에도 불구하고 소설은 그 불행의 원인을 탐색하기보다는 그 너머를 탐문한다. 모든 것을 잃은 이들이 서로의 위로가 된다는 것, 바로 그것이다. 서로의 결점을 말리고 설득하고 교정하려든다기보다 서로의 몰락을 지켜봐주고 격려해주고 함께 앓으려 한다는 것. 둘은 마흔셋 봄에 만나 10여 년을 함께 살다가 끝내 극한의 상태에 이

narrative constantly building to what the reader can only expect will be a tragic end, the story's tension heightens the tragedy of their eventual deaths.

"Spring Night's" principal characters, Yeong-gyeong and Su-hwan, are alcoholic and rheumatism-stricken respectively, "the al-rheu couple." Su-hwan enters the nursing home when his health begins to seriously deteriorate and Yeong-gyeong follows him both as a sign of solidarity and for her own needs. Yeong-gyeong and Su-hwan's previous twelve-years together was a time of tender vigilance and care with both partners reeling from personal failures and tragedies. While originally coming from starkly different worlds, Su-hwan and Yeong-gyeong meet for the first time at their friends' wedding and discover the similar wounds they carry from their first failed marriages. Su-hwan once worked in iron foundry in his twenties and owned his own in his thirties, but eventually had to file for bankruptcy. Shortly thereafter, his ex-wife betrayed him when Su-hwan follows his wife's recommendation that they divorce to protect their remaining assets. But Su-hwan's wife sells off all their assets and disappears, leaving Su-hwan heartbroken and severely financially delinquent.

른다. 둘 모두 손쓸 수 없이 상태가 악화된다. 금주증상에 시달리는 영경은 의사의 만류에도 불구하고 외출하고, 수환은 (재회를 확신하지 못하면서도) 그녀를 보내준다.

영경은 읍내의 편의점에서 술을 마신 후 모텔에서 정신을 잃은 채 발견된다. 그 사이 수환은 숨을 거둔다. 그의 곁에는 간병인 종우만이 있다. 종우는 수환의 병상에서 좋아하던 여자 이야기를 꺼낸다. 어긋난 연인, 치기어린 사랑의 징검다리 역할을 했던 여자(소연)를 보면 영경의 생각이 난다는 것. 소연은 종우가 암벽등반동호회에서 만난 은경의 환심을 사기 위해 잠깐 만났던 여자이다. 종우는 소연을 사귀는 척하면서 은경의 질투심을 자극하는 방식으로 은경의 마음을 얻었다. 얼마 후 종우는 계획대로 소연과 헤어지고 은경을 만나기 시작했다. 소연은 버림받고도 아무 원망 없이 종우의 곁에서 사라진다. 종우는 영경을 보면서 사라진 과거의 여자(소연)의 비극을 발견한다. 즉 홀로 남을 영경에게서 소연이 겪었을 동일한 비극의 잔영을 발견한 것. 임종의 자리에서 수없이 전화를 걸지만 영경의 핸드폰은 꺼져 있다. 수환의 심장이 멈추자 종우는 소리친다. "아줌마는 어쩔거야, 이제?"(84쪽) 영경이 의식불명의 상태

Meanwhile, Yeong-gyeong suffers from a tragedy no less devastating when, as moderately content Korean teacher and wife, she finds herself separated from her son after her ex-husband abducts their son and immigrates to a new country. This situation shortly thereafter drives Yeong-gyeong to alcoholism.

Although we are introduced to this couple at the tattered ends of their unhappy lives, the story chooses not to focus on explaining every minute detail of their unhappy conditions. Su-hwan becomes seriously ill because he is unable to receive health care in time because of his delinquent credit records. Yeong-gyeong becomes an alcoholic and chooses very early retirement after the loss of her child. And yet, the story does not dwell on the causes of their unhappy lives but searches for what lies beyond them. People who have lost everything can comfort each other. That is what this story is about. People trying to watch over and share each other's pain, choosing to encourage each other rather than trying to correct each other's problems or weaknesses. Yeong-gyeong and Su-hwan meet when they are both forty-three and live together for over a decade until their conditions become

로 요양원에 실려 왔을 때에는 수환의 장례식이 끝난 후였다. 영경은 가족조차 알아보지 못하는 상태로 한참을 지냈다. 그때 그녀는 수환의 존재조차 기억하지 못했다. 그녀를 지켜본 사람들은 이렇게 말했다(고 서술자는 전한다). "영경의 온전치 못한 정신이 수환을 보낼 때까지 죽을힘을 다해 견뎠다는 것을, 그리고 수환이 떠난 후에야 비로소 안심하고 죽어버렸다는 것을, 늙은 그들은 본능적으로 알았다."(86쪽) 상대보다 더 오래 살면서 상대의 죽음을 지킨다는 것, 이것은 분명히 사랑의 형식이다. 문제는 서로가 서로에게 그래야 한다는 것. 로미오와 줄리엣은 이것을 실천했고 「봄밤」의 늙은 애인들도 이것을 실천했다. 그녀가 모텔 방에서 혼자 끔찍한 죽음을 체험했을 때 그는 임종을 맞았고 그가 죽은 후에야 그녀는 다시 살아서도 죽은, 죽어버린 금치산자가 되었다.

"산다는 게 참 끔찍하다. 그렇지 않니?"(8쪽) 소설의 첫 문장이 갖는 의미는 여기서 발생한다. 영경은 기억을 잃은 채 몸만 되살아났다. 그러나 사랑하는 남자의 존재 자체를 잊게 된다. 가사상태를 벗어난 그녀를 과연 살았다고 말할 수 있을까. 영경은 두 번 죽는다. 처음

truly severe and their health deteriorates irrevocably. As Yeong-gyeong suffers from withdrawal symptoms, she takes her usual leave from the nursing home despite her doctor's advice. Su-hwan, meanwhile, willingly sends her away even while he is unsure if she will return before he dies. As the reader fears, Yeong-gyeong is found unconscious at a motel room when Su-hwan dies, only the caretaker Jong-u at his side. Before Su-hwan dies, Jong-u tells Su-hwan of his former girlfriend, a woman named So-yeon who played the role of a stepping-stone for his immature romantic life, a mismatched lover who reminded him of Yeong-gyeong. Jong-u tells Su-hwan that he primarily went out with So-yeon to approach another girl in whom he was really interested. By pretending to date So-yeon, Jong-u incited Eun-gyeong's jealousy and succeeded in winning her heart. Soon afterwards, Jong-u dumped So-yeon as planned and began his affair with Eun-gyeong. Meanwhile, So-yeon disappeared and without a word of protest. Jong-u finishes his tale by comparing the tragedy of his old lover, So-yeon, with that of Yeong-gyeong, who will also be left alone.

While Su-hwan's condition continues to deterio-

에 그녀는 가사상태에 빠졌고(실제의 그녀는 이때 죽었다), 몸만 살아났다. 언젠가 영경의 몸 역시 죽을 것이다. 그렇다면 이 두 죽음 사이에 끼인 영경의 몸은 어떤 의미를 갖는가. 영경의 몸은 저승으로 가지 못하고 이승에서 떠도는 영혼의 잔여라고 말해야 할지 모른다. 텅 빈 영경의 눈이 가르쳐주는 것은 이런 것이 아닐까? 죽은 원혼들이 이승에 남는 이유는 원한 때문이 아니다. 그것은 사랑 때문이다. 아직 기억할 게 남았다.

"내가 생각해봤는데 이 비유는 모든 사람에게 적용해볼 수 있을 거 같다. 분자에 그 사람의 좋은 점을 놓고 분모에 그 사람의 나쁜 점을 놓으면 그 사람의 값이 나오는 식이지. 아무리 장점이 많아도 단점이 많으면 그 값은 1보다 작고 그 역이면 1보다 크고."

"그러니까 1이 기준인 거네."

수환이 말했다. (…)

수환은 이렇게 말했지만, 실은 자신의 병이야말로 분모를 무한대로 늘리고 있어 자신의 값은 1보다 작은 건 물론이고 점점 0에 수렴되어가고 있는 중이라고 생각했다. 아니, 꼭 병 때문만이 아닐지도 몰랐다. (…) 그러

rate, Jong-u frantically calls Yeong-gyeong but to no avail. When Su-hwan's heart stops, Jong-u cries, "What's gonna happen to your wife, now?" The unconscious Yeong-gyeong is later taken to the nursing home but only after Su-hwan's funeral. Yeong-gyeong lives for a while longer, now unable to even recognize her own sisters. The story's narrator tells us, "The older people instinctively felt that Yeong-gyeong's impaired mind was trying desperately to stay alive until she could send Su-hwan away, and that it would only feel enough relief to die when Su-hwan had left for the other world." While it may be easy to make some judgments towards Su-hwan, one can certainly see outliving one's lover and watching over his or her death as one form of love. The problem arises, however, when both lovers want to do this for their lover. Thus follows the tragedies of Romeo and Juliet and "Spring Night." As Yeong-gyeong begins her solitary march towards death, Su-hwan actually does die, and only after this is Yeong-gyeong found alive, and yet, still dead in some sense, as she is declared legally incompetent.

"Life's an awful business, isn't it?" The meaning of this first sentence of the short story becomes clear

니 분모가 이토록 확 늘어가기 전에도 이미 분자의 숫자마저 미미했던 것이다.

(「봄밤」, 132~133쪽)

여기 수환의 사랑이 가진 애처로움이 드러난다. 수환이 술을 위한 그녀의 외출을 허락하는 것은 분자 하나라도 늘리려는 눈물겨운 노력이다. 이미 끝을 수락한 자만이 이를 알 수 있을 것이다. 사랑만이 죽음을 넘어선다. 죽음 때문에 상대의 소망을 제약한다면 그건 죽음의 분모가 사랑의 분자보다 크다는 뜻. 값은 1보다 작을 것이다. 사랑이 죽음을 넘어야 한다. 그것이 아무리 미미하더라도. 위대한 사랑의 서사는 이렇게 시작된다.

here. Yeong-gyeong is only revived physically. She forgets even her lover and so we might ask if we can really call her revival by that name? Yeong-gyeong dies twice. She loses consciousness first (her true death) and then is only revived physically. Even then, her body must die as well someday. What is the meaning of Yeong-gyeong's existence in between these two deaths? One might see her body as a sort of residue of her soul haunting this world. Isn't that what her vacant eyes show us? A spirit needs not stay in this world only because of its grudges. It can stay for love. Something that still should be remembered.

"I thought about this metaphor and it seems like you can apply it to everyone. If we think of someone's strong points as the numerator and their shortcomings as the denominator, we can find the value of that person. No matter how great a person's strength is, if his shortcomings are greater than his strengths, then, their value is less than 1, and vice versa."

"So, 1 is the standard," said Su-hwan...

Although Su-hwan spoke in this way, he thought that since his illness was extending his denominator to infinity, his value was not only smaller than 1, but also approaching zero. No, it wasn't even just his illness... Therefore, even before his denominator had begun expanding, the value of his numerator had become quite insignificant.

We see here how pitiful Su-hwan's love is. Su-hwan's act of sending Yeong-gyeong out so that she can drink is his pathetically sincere effort to increase the value of his numerator. It is something only someone who has already accepted his death can know and do. Only love trumps death. If he had limited his lover's wish for his own sake it would have meant his denominator of death had become greater than his numerator for love. His value would have been far smaller than 1. Love must always overcome death. No matter how much you have. This is where the great narrative of love begins.

비평의 목소리

Critical Acclaim

묘사체에서도 서술체에서도 한발 물러선 자리에 서서 작가 권여선 씨는 곳곳에다 아포리즘적 문체를 내세움으로써 주인공의 인중선의 또렷함처럼 작품의 논리성을 구축해놓았다.

김윤식

소재를 마름하는 독창성에서 보면 권여선은 단연 뛰어난 작가이다. 표면적으로 이끌어가는 이야기가 어떤 것이든, 작가는 항시 존재의 저 깊은 내면에 침전되어 있는 고통, 외로움, 공포를 조준하고 있고, 범상한 일상의 장면을 통해 느닷없이 그 깊은 틈을 드러낸다. 서영은

Standing a step aside in her descriptive or narrative style, Ms. Kwon Yeo-sun has scattered aphoristic sentences in this work and constructed a logicality as clear as the main character's philtrum line.

Kim Yun-sik

Kwon Yeo-sun is an author who has a strikingly original skill to craft her materials. Whatever story she narrates, she always seems to have the capacity to strike at the very pains, loneliness, and fear that lie in the depth of our beings. She unexpectedly reveals this depth through cracks in ordinary everyday scenes.

Seo Yeong-eun

권여선의 소설은 그리 명확하지도 친절하지도 거창하지도 않으며 오히려 의도를 드러내지 않고 감춘다. 그러나 드러내지 않은 것에서 우리는 결국 진실을 보게 되며 그런 것들은 오래 아름답다. 감춤의 미학이란 게 이런 걸까.

권지예

권여선의 소설이 일관된 하나의 명시적 주제나 메시지로 쉽게 수렴되지 않는 까닭은 여기에도 있으며, 형식의 이도한 부조화와 불균형이 또한 그것을 효과적으로 뒷받침한다. 그리고 권여선의 윤리감각은 바로 그 지점에서 작동한다. 그 윤리감각이란 물론 앞에서 보았듯 보통의 상식적 윤리감각을 뒤집는 윤리감각이다. 굳이 이른다면 그것을 두고 우리는 비(非)휴먼의 윤리라고 할 수 있을 것이다. 권여선의 소설은 그렇게, 그 어느 것으로도 환원할 수 없는 나름의 개성의 자리를 확보해 가는 중이다.

김영찬

지금 읽고 있는 소설이 어쩐지 바로 내 이야기를 하

Kwon Yeo-sun's stories are not that clear, kind, or grand. They hide their intentions rather than revealing them. However, this act of concealment ultimately leads us to truth, the beauty of which lasts for a long time. Might we call this "the aesthetic of concealment"?

Kwon Ji-ye

It is for this reason that Kwon Yeo-sun's works cannot be easily boiled down to a clear theme or message. Her stylistic disharmony and imbalance effectively support this. Kwon Yeo-sun's ethical sensibility operates exactly here. This ethical sensibility of hers is of course one that reverses the ordinary ethical sensibility as I have previously discussed. If we had to come up with a name for this kind of system of ethics, we might call it an inhuman code of ethics. Kwon Yeo-sun's fiction has secured a unique place in our literary scene, a place that cannot be reduced to any conventional ones.

Kim Yeong-chan

The feeling we get while reading a story, the feeling that we're reading our own stories—the

고 있는 듯한 느낌, 그것은 모든 소설의 본성이 아니라 좋은 소설에만 가능한 자질이다. 머리맡에 아껴두고 생각날 때마다 꺼내어 읽고 싶은 문장들로 가득찬 책을 읽었다. 그것은 아름다워서가 아니다. 이런 말이 허락된다면, 인생의 진실이 스며 있기 때문이다.

차미령

'아님'으로만 드러나는 장소. 권여선의 소설에서 실로 무수한 비자림을 찾아낼 수 있을 것이다. 그녀의 소설은 비밀을 폭로하는 소설이 아니라, 비밀이 거기에 있음을(다시 말해서 삶에 내재해 있음을) 알려주는 소설이다. 저 만곡의 끝이 흐릿하게 실종되었다. 요컨대 보이지 않는 것을, 보이지 않는 채로 보여주기, 그것이 바로 비자 숲의 기하학이다.

양윤의

각자의 아픔 속에서 이들의 고통은 균형을 이루며 그것을 서로 지켜보는 인내와 배려 속에서 사랑이 지켜지는 것이다. 더 이상 춥지 않지만 여전히 쓸쓸한 기운이 느껴지는 봄밤처럼 처연하고도 따뜻한 사랑 이야기가

ability of stories to make us feel this way is not a quality that belongs to just any story, but only to good ones. The book I've just finished reading was full of sentences that made me want to keep it on my bedside so that I can read them whenever I wanted. I feel this way about those sentences, not because they are beautiful, but because they are saturated with our lives' truth.

Cha Mi-ryeong

A place appearing only through its negation. We can find numerous Bija Tree Groves in Kwon Yeo-sun's works. Her stories do not reveal secrets, but let us know that the secrets are there (in other words, inherent in our lives). The end of a curve vanishes gradually. In short, they show what is invisible as what is invisible—that is the geometry of Bija Tree Groves.

Yang Yun-ui

Their pains balance each other in their respective sufferings, and they are able to maintain their love by patiently and tenderly watching each other handle their pains. This is a mournful, warm love story like a spring night that is no longer cold, but still a

여기 있다.

조연정

little chilly.

Jo Yeon-jeong

권여선

권여선은 1965년 경북 안동에서 태어났으며 본명은 권희선이다. 서울대학교 국문과와 동대학원을 졸업했다. 1996년 장편 『푸르른 틈새』로 상상문학상을 수상하며 등단했다. 2004년 『처녀치마』를 출간한 이후 본격적으로 권여선식 캐릭터, 즉 집요하고 억척스러운 인물이 등장하는 작품들을 선보이기 시작한다. 예를 들어 음식을 먹는 디테일한 묘사에서 인물의 집요한 성격을 뽑아내는데 이때 식성은 그 자체로 하나의 캐릭터가 된다. 두 번째 창작집 『분홍 리본의 시절』에서 권여선 특유의 솔직하고 거침없는 문체로 개인의 상처와 일상의 균열을 형상화하여 좋은 반응을 얻었다. 2007년 「약콩이 끓는 동안」으로 오영수문학상을, 2008년 「사랑을 믿다」로 이상문학상을, 2012년 오랜만에 낸 두 번째 장편인 『레가토』로 한국일보문학상을 수상했다.

Kwon Yeo-sun

Kwon Yeo-sun was born in Andong, Korea in 1965 as Kwon Hee-sun. She received a B.A. and M.A. in Korean literature from Seoul National University. She made her literary debut in 1996, when her novel *Blue Opening* won the Sangsang [Imagination] Literary Award. Since *Cheonyeochima*, published in 2004, Kwon Yeo-sun began to feature obsessive and persistent, "Kwon Yeo-sun-style" characters in her novels and stories. For example, in her detailed description of someone eating, we are presented with pure obsession, to the degree that appetite itself becomes a character. Her second short story collection, *Pink Ribbon Period,* received a glowing critical response by depicting personal wounds and everyday cracks in character in her characteristically frank and straightforward style. She won the 2007 Oh Yeong-su Literary Award for "While the Medicine Beans Are Boiling," the 2008 Yi Sang Literary Award for "Believing in Love," and the 2012 *Hankook Ilbo* Literary Award for her first novel *Legato*.

번역 **전승희** Translated by Jeon Seung-hee

전승희는 서울대학교와 하버드대학교에서 영문학과 비교문학으로 박사 학위를 받았으며, 현재 하버드대학교 한국학 연구소의 연구원으로 재직하며 아시아 문예 계간지 《ASIA》 편집위원으로 활동 중이다. 현대 한국문학 및 세계문학을 다룬 논문을 다수 발표했으며, 바흐친의 『장편소설과 민중언어』, 제인 오스틴의 『오만과 편견』 등을 공역했다. 1988년 한국여성연구소의 창립과 《여성과 사회》의 창간에 참여했고, 2002년부터 보스턴 지역 피학대 여성을 위한 단체인 '트랜지션하우스' 운영에 참여해 왔다. 2006년 하버드대학교 한국학 연구소에서 '한국 현대사와 기억'을 주제로 한 워크숍을 주관했다.

Jeon Seung-hee is a member of the Editorial Board of ***ASIA***, and a Fellow at the Korea Institute, Harvard University. She received a Ph.D. in English Literature from Seoul National University and a Ph.D. in Comparative Literature from Harvard University. She has presented and published numerous papers on modern Korean and world literature. She is also a co-translator of Mikhail Bakhtin's ***Novel and the People's Culture*** and Jane Austen's ***Pride and Prejudice***. She is a founding member of the Korean Women's Studies Institute and of the biannual Women's Studies' journal ***Women and Society*** (1988), and she has been working at 'Transition House,' the first and oldest shelter for battered women in New England. She organized a workshop entitled "The Politics of Memory in Modern Korea" at the Korea Institute, Harvard University, in 2006. She also served as an advising committee member for the Asia-Africa Literature Festival in 2007 and for the POSCO Asian Literature Forum in 2008.

감수 **데이비드 윌리엄 홍** Edited by David William Hong

데이비드 윌리엄 홍은 미국 일리노이주 시카고에서 태어났다. 일리노이대학교에서 영문학을, 뉴욕대학교에서 영어교육을 공부했다. 지난 2년간 서울에 거주하면서 처음으로 한국인과 아시아계 미국인 문학에 깊이 몰두할 기회를 가졌다. 현재 뉴욕에서 거주하며 강의와 저술 활동을 한다.

David William Hong was born in 1986 in Chicago, Illinois. He studied English Literature at the University of Illinois and English Education at New York University. For the past two years, he lived in Seoul, South Korea, where he was able to immerse himself in Korean and Asian-American literature for the first time. Currently, he lives in New York City, teaching and writing.

바이링궐 에디션 한국 대표 소설 055
봄밤

2014년 3월 7일 초판 1쇄 인쇄 | 2014년 3월 14일 초판 1쇄 발행

지은이 권여선 | **옮긴이** 전승희 | **펴낸이** 김재범
감수 데이비드 윌리엄 홍 | **기획** 정은경, 전성태, 이경재
편집 정수인, 이은혜 | **관리** 박신영 | **디자인** 이춘희
펴낸곳 (주)아시아 | **출판등록** 2006년 1월 27일 제406-2006-000004호
주소 서울특별시 동작구 서달로 161-1(흑석동 100-16)
전화 02.821.5055 | **팩스** 02.821.5057 | **홈페이지** www.bookasia.org
ISBN 979-11-5662-002-0 (set) | 979-11-5662-012-9 (04810)
값은 뒤표지에 있습니다.

Bi-lingual Edition Modern Korean Literature 055
Spring Night

Written by Kwon Yeo-sun | **Translated by** Jeon Seung-hee
Published by Asia Publishers | 161-1, Seodal-ro, Dongjak-gu, Seoul, Korea
Homepage Address www.bookasia.org | **Tel**. (822).821.5055 | **Fax**. (822).821.5057
First published in Korea by Asia Publishers 2014
ISBN 979-11-5662-002-0 (set) | 979-11-5662-012-9 (04810)

〈바이링궐 에디션 한국 대표 소설〉 작품 목록(1~45)

도서출판 아시아는 지난 반세기 동안 한국에서 나온 가장 중요하고 첨예한 문제의식을 가진 작가들의 작품들을 선별하여 총 105권의 시리즈를 기획하였다. 하버드 한국학 연구원 및 세계 각국의 우수한 번역진들이 참여하여 외국인들이 읽어도 어색함이 느껴지지 않는 손색없는 번역으로 인정받았다. 이 시리즈는 세계인들에게 문학 한류의 지속적인 힘과 가능성을 입증하는 전집이 될 것이다.

바이링궐 에디션 한국 대표 소설 set 1

분단 Division

01 병신과 머저리-**이청준** The Wounded-**Yi Cheong-jun**
02 어둠의 혼-**김원일** Soul of Darkness-**Kim Won-il**
03 순이삼촌-**현기영** Sun-i Samch'on-**Hyun Ki-young**
04 엄마의 말뚝 1-**박완서** Mother's Stake I-**Park Wan-suh**
05 유형의 땅-**조정래** The Land of the Banished-**Jo Jung-rae**

산업화 Industrialization

06 무진기행-**김승옥** Record of a Journey to Mujin-**Kim Seung-ok**
07 삼포 가는 길-**황석영** The Road to Sampo-**Hwang Sok-yong**
08 아홉 켤레의 구두로 남은 사내-**윤흥길** The Man Who Was Left as Nine Pairs of Shoes-**Yun Heung-gil**
09 돌아온 우리의 친구-**신상웅** Our Friend's Homecoming-**Shin Sang-ung**
10 원미동 시인-**양귀자** The Poet of Wŏnmi-dong-**Yang Kwi-ja**

여성 Women

11 중국인 거리-**오정희** Chinatown-**Oh Jung-hee**
12 풍금이 있던 자리-**신경숙** The Place Where the Harmonium Was-**Shin Kyung-sook**
13 하나코는 없다-**최윤** The Last of Hanak'o-**Ch'oe Yun**
14 인간에 대한 예의-**공지영** Human Decency-**Gong Ji-young**
15 빈처-**은희경** Poor Man's Wife-**Eun Hee-kyung**

바이링궐 에디션 한국 대표 소설 set 2

자유 Liberty

16 필론의 돼지-**이문열** Pilon's Pig-**Yi Mun-yol**
17 슬로우 불릿-**이대환** Slow Bullet-**Lee Dae-hwan**
18 직선과 독가스-**임철우** Straight Lines and Poison Gas-**Lim Chul-woo**
19 깃발-**홍희담** The Flag-**Hong Hee-dam**
20 새벽 출정-**방현석** Off to Battle at Dawn-**Bang Hyeon-seok**

사랑과 연애 Love and Love Affairs

21 별을 사랑하는 마음으로-**윤후명** With the Love for the Stars-**Yun Hu-myong**
22 목련공원-**이승우** Magnolia Park-**Lee Seung-u**
23 칼에 찔린 자국-**김인숙** Stab-**Kim In-suk**
24 회복하는 인간-**한강** Convalescence-**Han Kang**
25 트렁크-**정이현** In the Trunk-**Jeong Yi-hyun**

남과 북 South and North

26 판문점-**이호철** Panmunjom-**Yi Ho-chol**
27 수난 이대-**하근찬** The Suffering of Two Generations-**Ha Geun-chan**
28 분지-**남정현** Land of Excrement-**Nam Jung-hyun**
29 봄 실상사-**정도상** Spring at Silsangsa Temple-**Jeong Do-sang**
30 은행나무 사랑-**김하기** Gingko Love-**Kim Ha-kee**

바이링궐 에디션 한국 대표 소설 set 3

서울 Seoul

31 눈사람 속의 검은 항아리-**김소진** The Dark Jar within the Snowman-**Kim So-jin**
32 오후, 가로지르다-**하성란** Traversing Afternoon-**Ha Seong-nan**
33 나는 봉천동에 산다-**조경란** I Live in Bongcheon-dong-**Jo Kyung-ran**
34 그렇습니까? 기린입니다-**박민규** Is That So? I'm A Giraffe-**Park Min-gyu**
35 성탄특선-**김애란** Christmas Specials-**Kim Ae-ran**

전통 Tradition

36 무자년의 가을 사흘-**서정인** Three Days of Autumn, 1948-**Su Jung-in**
37 유자소전-**이문구** A Brief Biography of Yuja-**Yi Mun-gu**
38 향기로운 우물 이야기-**박범신** The Fragrant Well-**Park Bum-shin**
39 월행-**송기원** A Journey under the Moonlight-**Song Ki-won**
40 협죽도 그늘 아래-**성석제** In the Shade of the Oleander-**Song Sok-ze**

아방가르드 Avant-garde

41 아겔다마-**박상륭** Akeldama-**Park Sang-ryoong**
42 내 영혼의 우물-**최인석** A Well in My Soul-**Choi In-seok**
43 당신에 대해서-**이인성** On You-**Yi In-seong**
44 회색 時-**배수아** Time In Gray-**Bae Su-ah**
45 브라운 부인-**정영문** Mrs. Brown-**Jung Young-moon**